Tezmec stood frozen. . .

A burning phosphorescence—like the kind seen at sea that hovers over the masts of ships—enveloped the sacrificial stone. The jade mask glowed and seemed to throw out rays of emerald light. Tezmec held the still-beating heart in his hand. It was throbbing, moving. The golden knife dropped from Tezmec's grasp when another hand covered his.

Casca, his body enveloped in the green fire of the sea, stood holding Tezmec's hand stationary over the altar fire. And then Casca took his own beating heart out of the priest's hand.

"It takes a god to kill a god, and my time is not yet come.

"I am Casca. I am the Quetza.

"I am God!"

Charter Books by Barry Sadler

CASCA #1: THE ETERNAL MERCENARY
CASCA #2: GOD OF DEATH
CASCA #3: THE WAR LORD
CASCA #4: PANZER SOLDIER
CASCA #5: THE BARBARIAN
CASCA #6: THE PERSIAN
CASCA #7: THE DAMNED
CASCA #8: SOLDIER OF FORTUNE
CASCA #9: THE SENTINEL
CASCA #10: THE CONQUISTADOR
CASCA #11: THE LEGIONNAIRE
CASCA #12: THE AFRICAN MERCENARY
CASCA #13: THE ASSASSIN
CASCA #14: THE PHOENIX
CASCA #15: THE PIRATE
CASCA #16: DESERT MERCENARY (coming in February 1986)

GOD OF DEATH

#2

BARRY
SADLER

CHARTER BOOKS, NEW YORK

CASCA #2: GOD OF DEATH

A Charter Book / published by arrangement with
the author

PRINTING HISTORY
Charter edition / December 1979
Tenth printing / December 1985

ISBN: 0-441-09335-3

Charter Books are published by The Berkley Publishing Group,
200 Madison Avenue, New York, New York 10016.
PRINTED IN THE UNITED STATES OF AMERICA

CASCA:
GOD OF DEATH

PROLOGUE

Casca came to the Rhine at the same spot where he had fought his first battle against the German tribesmen known as the Suevii; the grass always seemed to be a little richer where blood had been spilled. In his mind he could almost make out the outlines of the fight, a smaller patch of green a hundred yards distant where the young men of the cavalry unit assigned to Casca's unit had been pulled from their horses by long-hooked poles and had their throats slit with fishknives while they lay on the ground. That barbarian ambush had almost been successful. Only the legion's automatic response to danger and the immediate forming of the square had saved them all from being butchered and having their heads stuck on poles outside the longhouses of the barbaric tribesmen from across the Rhine.

Casca walked slowly, memories rushing upon him. Stopping, he bent over and picked up a piece of metal protruding from the earth. It was the handle of a knife, a knife stuck in something. Tugging gently, Casca freed it. The rusty blade came forth, almost completely eaten away but still strong enough to hold the piece of human skull it had penetrated so many years ago. *Ours? Or theirs?* Casca mused. He hooked his pack up higher and looked in the direction of the river. He walked toward it, his footsteps taking him back to that first battle when he was young and the copper taste of piss-blinding fear was in his mouth. He knew that beneath his feet were the bones of men whom he had known and served with, some friends, some not, but all comrades. *The legion . . . the legion . . . my only true home . . . my father and my mother. . . . Here is where I killed my first man over a hundred and fifty years ago. The wheel turns. As I told the leader of the caravan out of Anatolia before we headed for Damascus, the wheels of the gods grind slow, yet they grind exceedingly fine. Everything is as it was and will be. The only exception is me. I am what I was and apparently always will be until the Jew comes again. I am the continuation of myself. Shit, where the hell did I learn to talk like that? Continuation my ass. I am what I am, and perhaps I get a little maudlin now and then. But life is still interesting. There are yet places to go, people to meet, women to love . . . and leave. . . .*

Casca drew himself erect, his hand on his belt. He looked across the river. *The Jew said it: What I am, that I shall be. Good enough. I am Casca, soldier of the legions, part-time slave—but I exist.* Cogito, ergo sum. *I will beat the Jew yet. My fortunes lie in front of me . . . in life and adventure.*

Certainly I get feelings of sympathy for myself now and then, but, as He said, I am what I am. Therefore I shall live the life that my destiny demands. But as my own man.

Absorbed in his interior monologue, Casca had reached the river.

The Rhine, dark and swift, flowed before him. He knelt at the same spot where he had slaked his thirst in the then bloody waters of that battle so long ago . . . his battle thirst after the Suevii had broken and run, and the legionnaires had slaughtered them all the way to the river and even in it. The passing face of a young German boy ran before Casca's eyes . . . and faded. One he had killed? It grew hard to recall thom all after a while. Casca sat by the bank of the great river looking across to where no Roman in his right mind would want to be. Germania. *Terra incognita.* The unknown lands of the fiercest tribesmen on earth. The Germans and the Parthians were the only peoples to stand against the might of Imperial Rome. But the Parthians were cultured and rich, with not only the heritage of the great Persian Empire, but with the sophistication of their first conquerors, the Greeks, under the young warrior, Alexander. The Germans were something else. Casca had the feeling they would always be a pain in the ass to the rest of the world no matter how civilized they might eventually become on the surface. They had born in them, and nurtured by the first taste of their mothers' milk, a lust for life that fulfilled itself only in battle.

By all the demons of whatever reality there are, it seems as if the sage Shiu Lao Tze was right.

Everything is a great circle and repeats itself like that endless line of slaves in the mines of Greece, never ending, always coming back to the beginning. Or is it the end? Perhaps beginning and ending are both the same.

The night was close upon him, and the water looked too damned cold for swimming across in the dark. Tomorrow is time enough. Building a small fire, Casca waited, letting the warmth of the red embers reach deep within him. The piece of donkey meat he was cooking crackled and sizzled. The rich smell of the roasting meat made his mouth salivate. In anticipation, he smacked his lips. Ahh! There's nothing like a nice hot piece of young ass to set a man's mouth watering. . . .

As the meat turned crisp and juicy, Casca reached over and cut off a slice and filled his mouth with the strong taste of young ass. He gulped the meat down, pulled his cloak around him, rolled over, and went to sleep facing the fire.

Tomorrow, Germany . . .

When the dawn came and Casca awoke, there was the same type fog rolling across the river as had surrounded the ghostlike images of the Suevii floating across the Rhine on logs so many years ago. But this time it was Casca's turn to enter the whirling waters.

The coals of his fire had long since died. Grumbling as he rose, he walked to the water's edge, scratching his ass. He farted and joined his stream with that of the mighty river. Going back to his campsite, he stirred the dead coals hopefully and looked questioningly at a piece of the donkey flesh that remained, but it was now black and charred. Restraining a belch, he mumbled, "No way. There's no way I'm going to eat a piece of cold burned ass this early in the morning."

The ground fog swirled around him and the trees. The dawn became day. The rising sun burned off the mist, a few rays breaking through the surrounding trees to give a sense of impending warmth.

"Well, shit," he said aloud, looking at the river, "I might as well get it over with. The sooner I get across, the sooner I can dry off." He dragged a log to the river's edge, tied his gear, a chunk of donkey meat, and his pack to it, and shoved off into the frigid, dark waters, gingerly at first as he waded in, cursing at the icy cold. "Ooh! Ah! Damn, that's cold!" As the Rhine slowly advanced up his legs, his scrotum tried to climb up even higher to avoid the chilling advance, but, as nature wills it, his balls could only go up so far. Then he was in, and the coldness became warm as he struck off and began paddling across, letting the current take him. It really didn't make a damn where he landed, so he let the river do the work.

The waters finally took him to where his feet could touch bottom. Groaning, he pushed the log to the edge of the bank and began to take his gear from it before leaving the water himself.

"Ho, little man! What do you here?"

The speaker, unexpected as he was, seemed to exemplify that popular image of German barbarism. He stood six-foot-three, and he was two hundred and fifty pounds of meat-stuffed flesh if he was an ounce. He wore a horned helmet, and his sweeping mustache would have made a walrus proud.

"Ho, little man!" he repeated, his voice the thundering bellow of an oversize Germanic ox. "Do you ashore come? I can see that you are not of the tribes, so therefore you must pay before entering this land. As I am a reasonable man, I will take only your pack and weapons, leaving you your clothes. They would not fit anyway. Fair enough? Or do you wish to dispute me over the matter?" With this he drew a monstrous long sword that must have weighed forty pounds and swung it easily through the air, the slicing blade whistling. He used just one hand and then brought the sword down, resting the point at his thong-wrapped feet.

"Well, what will it be, my wet little titmouse? Though you are larger than most of your sickly ilk, I can see by your rags that you are a Latin. May Wotan piss in your soup."

Oh, no, thought Casca. *This is all I need to start the day off.* Getting a firm footing on the slippery bottom, he raised himself up to a full height of five-foot-ten—which still seemed small, woefully small, in comparison to the huge barbarian.

"Now, listen to me, lard guts," he said in German. "I have had just about enough of your mouth and this river. Take your large, overstuffed carcass away and leave me in peace, or I'll ruin your love life by braiding your legs. *Verstand, sheiss kopf?*"

"*Shit head* you dare call me? Glam Tyrsbjörn a shit head? Come out of the water, you dago mouse, and I'll teach you some manners."

"Piss on you, fur mouth. I'm no dummy. If you want a piece of my ass, let's make it even. Either you back off and let me out of the river, or come in and get your feet wet, turnip dick."

"Turnip dick!" Glam turned first red, then white, then purple with rage. Stamping his fur-wrapped feet like a human version of the old forest ox of the Aurochs, he bellowed, "I would come in after you, but I am no fish and cannot swim. So come out where I can put my hands on you. I am going to shove my right fist up your ass so far that I will grab you by the jawbone and pull you inside out."

"Big deal, big mouth," Casca scoffed. "Sure you're tough with that oversize meat cleaver. If you didn't have that, you'd be like a castratto—which you may be anyway. I keep hearing your whimpering turn into a falsetto, you louse-ridden eunuch."

"By the bones of Ymir from which Odin and his brothers created the world, I will show you that I need nothing but my own hands to complete your education, Roman boy!" With that, Glam threw his monstrous long sword from him with such force that it almost severed a two-foot pine, the point burying itself in the wood. "There, you lousy dago! Now will you come out and fight?"

"You got it, sausage breath." Casca splashed his way out of the river while Glam stomped and waited, chewing his mustache in anticipation of settling the afront made to his honor. Turnip dick indeed!

As Casca came out, Glam turned and threw a long, looping punch that Casca easily dodged. Using the art of the yellow sage Shiu Tze, Casca blocked with his right arm and gave a quick, inside snap kick to the balls. Glam, between clenched teeth, tried with both hands to comfort his bruised groin. While he was involved with coddling himself, Casca went into a reverse roundhouse kick with his heel that knocked the big German into the Rhine unconscious, face down. Bubbles of air started welling up as the German drowned. Casca watched for a second, then, grumbling about being a sucker, he waded out into the river and grabbed the soggy tribesman by the hair and raised his face out of the water. Holding Glam by the hair of the head with one hand, Casca began a firm cracking slap across the face with the other. Glam sputtered, spitting out a quantity of the sacred Rhine.

"Enough!" he burbled. "Enough! I surrender. I'm your slave. Just get me out of the water."

"All right, but one wrong twitch and I'll do what I said about your legs."

"No, master. I, Glam, son of Halfdan the Ganger, may be many things, but I keep my word. You win. Just remove me from this miserable river and set my feet on solid earth."

The Norseman's helmet had gone to the bottom, so Casca got a firmer grip on the shoulder-length hair and hauled Glam to where he could pull himself out of the river to the edge of the bank and lie down. This the German did, his lungs trying to turn themselves inside out. While he finished this process, Casca returned and hauled his gear out. Sitting on a moss-covered log, he took a dry rag and began to wipe down his short sword, for he was a warrior, and a warrior takes care of his weapons.

By the time Casca had finished cleaning his gear and drying himself off as best he could, the sun was giving indication that the day would be bright and warm. Glam drew himself erect and strode to stand in front of Casca. Tensing, Casca took a firmer grip on his blade, but Glam suddenly dropped to his face and lay down in front of Casca. Taking Casca's right foot, he set it on top of his head. "I swear by the Aesir and Odin Allfather that I am your man in all things until you release me from my pledge."

Tossing Casca's foot off, Glam jumped back. "Well, now that that is over, where do we go from here, master?"

Casca looked up at the fur-draped and water-dripping giant. He grumbled, but there was a laugh behind his voice trying to break through. "For someone who's just made himself a slave, you're not very damn humble."

"Humble?" Glam asked in surprise. "Why in the name of the sacred oak should I be humble? I am the finest fighter and bravest man in the northlands from Scandia to the Danube. Sure, I'm your slave. But who said anything about being humble?" He beckoned to Casca. "Come by the fire, little master, and take the chill of the river off your bones. We'll take a bite of your smoked ass, and you will learn how fortunate you are to have a man like myself as a friend and companion."

"Friend and companion? What the Hades happened to your being my slave?"

Nonplussed, Glam continued somewhat testily, "Well, if you want to be rigid in your thinking, that's so. But I thought we might modify our relationship a little bit. It is only because I find myself liking you in spite of your parentage that I would be willing to make such an offer, because, knowing myself, I know that I would be an unhappy slave and as such would most likely cause you a great deal of trouble and concern. But as a friend and companion —Ahh!—that's something else. In that happy condition I would put all my intelligence and resources at your disposal. Now, wouldn't that be better than having an unhappy slave that you couldn't trust?"

By the time the big German had ended his monologue Casca was desperately trying to control a fit of laughter. Choking it back, he cleared his throat. "Good enough, my monstrous friend. We will be comrades until the time when our roads must part. Until then, we will be true to one another in our actions and trust. Is it agreed?" He held out his hand.

Glam nodded his head vigorously up and down. "Aye, Roman, that it is. And think not that I am ungrateful for your releasing me from my bonds on slavery, for certainly I was miserable all the time of my servitude."

Casca laughed out loud in spite of himself. "By Mithra, man, you were a slave for only less than an hour. How much misery could you acquire in that short a time?"

Glam responded in wounded tones, his mustache starting to bristle up. "It is not the length of bondage. It is the emotional pain of the condition that counts. And I—" he visibly swelled "—I have the soul of a poet. The soul, if—regrettably—not the words."

"Stop. Enough already, you great barbarian. I accept your reasoning. Just spare me the story." Glam nodded in agreement, and Casca went on. It was best to get their relationship straight from the beginning. "First things first," he said. "My name is

Casca. And I'm no one's dummy. I've been around a long time—longer than you might think. I know most of the tricks of the trade. In fact, I've invented a few of them. I have been a soldier in the legions, and I have hired out my sword as a mercenary to those who could pay the price. The only thing I won't do is fight a fight I don't believe in. There is enough action around that I don't think we have to sell our souls to the shitmongers. So, if you want to come with me, let's understand things. I am the boss, and we play by my rules." He locked eyes with the big German. The intent with which he spoke allowed for no smart answers. His tone was absolutely serious.

Uneasily, Glam looked away for a moment. There was something about this stranger that was disturbing, something for which there was no ready answer. A power? What could it be? But he looked back full in Casca's eyes and said, "Good enough. You are the leader until our road ends."

The road Casca and Glam took was, for the most part, a good one. The two rapidly found a fondness for each other that went far beyond the relationship of master and servant. Glam, with his boisterous humor, was almost as good as he thought he was—though he never got used to the idea that the smaller Roman had whipped him without even using weapons. That summer of A.D. 210 they walked through the great dank forests of Germania. Casca kept his Roman armor out of sight in his kit bag. The sight of the hated Roman cuirass might lead to more trouble than they wanted. The trail through the woods had the rich smell of life, of green and growing things. The sun broke through the treetops with shining, hazy blades of light and lit up the floor of the forest so that it glowed with green fire. The feel of such spots was most welcome for in the morning and in the afternoon a chill would come.

Glam taught Casca the way of the Norsemen. Here were few towns in the style of those found in the lands and provinces of Imperial Rome. But there was no shortage of people; they merely chose not to live one on top of the other. Glam rambled through these woods resembling in his fur robes and shuffling gait one of the brown bears that inhabited these regions. He was a strange partner for Casca the Roman, this northern barbarian, but they became friends and comrades. Their lives were intertwined and their loyalties tested by battles and time. Glam told Casca of immense lands that ran from the frozen sea to the mountains that held up the sky. Here the tribes roamed at will, and those with great chieftains had tens of thousands of warriors at their call. To Glam this was the best of all lands, the women more beautiful, the men braver, the beer stronger. The two wound their way slowly, bearing north, ever northward.

Glam grumbled about the way the tribes on the Roman sides of the Rhine, the Danube, and the Elbe had become but pale shadows of their former glory when they had been worthy foes. Now they aped the Roman in all things and were, to Glam's thinking, little better than falsetto-voiced castratti like all those from Italia—present company excluded, of course, he hastily added as he caught Casca thoughtfully eyeing his crotch. Glam instantly recalled Casca's threat to braid his legs and thus end his sex life . . . to the detriment of untapped legions of fair maids. . . .

Glam changed the subject and went more into a travelogue. Indicating the general area to the east with a broad sweep of his hand, he said in his most officious voice: "There. Over there are trackless lands that have never seen the foot of man. Others where only the wildest savages live—half man, half horse—great hordes of them . . . small gnomes whose legs are bent so badly they can hardly walk on the ground because they've spent so much time on horseback that their legs have grown crooked. And there are others almost as bad. Hundreds of thousands of them. Still they are only specks on the great steppes of Scythia and the even more desolate region that runs untold leagues beyond. Mark my words, Casca. One day we will have more than our share of trouble coming out of the east. If those devils ever start to move, they won't leave enough grass behind them to feed a family of grasshoppers."

"You have seen these people you talk of, Glam?"

"Aye, Lord Casca, I have. Several came as emissaries once to the king of the Alani when I was renting him the use of my sword as a bodyguard for a while. He was having family problems at the time and didn't trust his own men too closely. Yes, these ugly bowlegged little bastards even conducted their treaties from horseback. I got one stewed on fermented mare's milk—which they drink—and learned a little from him. They are indeed going to be moving west sometime. Now there is only a trickle this way, but, from the little bastard I talked to, I learned that they have their problems, too. Even greater and more terrible tribes are pushing them out of the lands they inhabit on the endless prairies near the wall, 'The Wall That Goes on Forever'—at least that's what he called it, though I am sure he is a bit of a liar. A wall that goes on forever! Indeed!" Glam snorted through his mustache at the idea. "From what I saw of those beasts they would be extremely unpleasant to have as neighbors. They have absolutely no sense of appreciation for the finer things of life as we of the northlands do."

Glam squashed a particularly fat louse and blinked as the body popped between his thick nails. He ambled on, unaware that Casca was sore put to keep from breaking out in laughter at Glam's wounded sense of propriety and sensitivity.

He was the mainstay when Casca met Lida at Ragnar's Hold.

Lida.

Now there was something strange.

Glam knew all about women—as women. And he expected Casca to be like himself. But the thing between Casca and Lida, golden-haired, lovely, beautiful young Lida, daughter of Ragnar the Brutal One, was like one of those romances the poets sang about. From the moment their eyes touched, something passed between them that was above and beyond the normal way of man and maid. Old Ragnar found out, of course. Old Ragnar, to whom even a daughter was only property that no man dared touch. In his insane rage when Lida had the temerity to stand up to him and say, "I have eyes only for Casca," he had blinded her with a torch jerked from the wall, crying, "Then, by Thor, you'll have no eyes!" And when he ordered Casca tossed into a dungeon to starve to death, even his hardened warriors were so frightened by Ragnar's enormous rage and brutal act toward his own daughter that they carried out his orders, smothering Casca by sheer weight of numbers before the Roman could find out what had occurred in Ragnar's rooms—for they sensed that if he knew, even the force of the Aesir would not hold him back.

Once secured in the dungeon, though, Casca had been told—by Ragnar himself whose sense of vengeance was as strong as his hate. Casca raged, but even his great strength was of no avail against such great stones as enclosed the dungeon.

Old Ragnar was a mean old shit, so used to having his way that he never doubted he would always have it. Casca stayed in the dungeon for six months until one day Ragnar, sure that Casca was long dead, gave orders for a new prisoner to be lodged there. But when the door opened, Casca came out, naked as a jaybird, nothing but bones and skin. He had eaten all his clothing—even the lacings on his leggings—along with every insect, bug, and rat that dared showed itself in the black cell. Water he licked from the walls where it condensed in drops. Surely there was not enough to keep any man alive two weeks, much less six months, but Casca lived.

He snapped the jailer's neck with one of his strange blows, took the man's weapon, and like some weird nightmare of a man, wild beard falling from his chin, he sought out and killed old Ragnar at his own table where the brutal old bastard was entertaining guests. Glam had been there, having found himself local employment in order to keep an eye on Lida. Casca had told him to wait, no matter how long, and from the things Glam had seen on the trail, he believed the strange Roman. Joyfully, Glam shouted and reached for his sword when this filthy, starved, weird-looking wretch leaped into the middle of Ragnar's table with an axe in one hand and a leg of mutton in the other. He scared the crap out of everyone there, sending all but the sturdiest warriors running for their lives. They thought he must surely be some demon out of the netherworld sent by Loki. Glam roared with amusement as he watched Casca bashing out the brains of old Ragnar with the leg of meat while whacking two of the household bodyguards with the axe—and never missing a bite. Glam's own joyful efforts to assist Casca helped speed up the demise of the few who dared resist them. For the rest, the sight of the lord being debrained by a hairy, filthy skeleton of a demon wielding a leg of mutton and a battleaxe was too much. They fled the house, leaving Ragnar's Hold to the madman. They were afraid of nothing human. But this was too much. . . .

Forty years ago Lida was a golden-haired thing of light and silver. She moved like a summer breeze. . . .

Old Glam snuffled in his beard. Even sightless she knew every inch of the Hold that was then hers and Casca's. Casca became the Lord of the Hold, and none disputed it—and lived. . . .

Wiping a tear from his eyes, Glam thought, *I loved her, too, Casca. And she was beautiful to the end. A lovely lady with a heart for everyone and everything. Especially you, you lousy dago.*" This had been a good place for them. It took only a few fights around the neighborhood to show that this was no place to muck about with.

Glam shivered as he saw again those clear white sightless eyes of Lady Lida. Forty years and she never knew Casca's secret. . . . *That's the greatest miracle of all. I never saw a man love anyone as much as he did her. When she died, I thought for a moment he was going to have himself buried with her. But then he's a strange little bastard. Those touched by the gods always are. He has his fate to follow, and personally I don't envy him. But the years have been good.*

Laughing in his mead, Glam chuckled and muttered softly: "What was it he first called me? Turnip dick? Ha!"

ONE

Dr. Julius Goldman entered the magnificent doors leading into the sacrosanct interior of the Boston Museum of History. He was late. His footsteps clattered over the polished marble floor, his own sense of urgency seeming to precede him with the echoing sound as he passed the priceless relics of antiquity, the emblems of vanished civilizations. Vases from China. Amphorae from Greece. Each a lonely and mute survivor of its past. Ancient weapons. Time-forgotten ornaments. Each seemed ready to speak, to tell some dark secret of the ages. Despite his haste, Goldman felt the atmosphere of the museum seeping into his brain.

He turned left down an exhibit hall leading toward his destination, the newly acquired exhibit of Mesoamerican art from Mexico. On the way, though, he approached a well-used and exquisitely preserved set of Roman gladiatorial armor, its great helmet and famed Roman short sword hanging expectantly in the silent museum as though suspended in time. Involuntarily his steps slowed, and he stopped in front of the carefully mounted pieces. A gash ran along the belly of the armor, exposing the leather wrappings beneath. Goldman wondered how the man who had been wearing it had come out. As he stood before the armor, images flashed in his brain, and a feeling of second sight came over him, a tumbling of memories lost and found and then gone again before awareness. He saw in his mind's eye a massive stadium filled with people crying for blood. He saw men wearing the armor of the Secutor and the Mirimillone locked in mortal combat, straining to let the lifeblood out of their opponents, and not with any reluctance for they were glorying in their strength. Goldman felt himself part of the Roman games. The smell of the blood-soaked sand stank in his nostrils.

He turned from the armor and entered the Aztec exhibit. The museum had just opened and was practically empty, but Goldman had been here the previous week and he recalled with particular distaste seeing two aficionados of this pre-Columbian culture standing before these exhibits, indulging themselves in a form of controlled, vicarious, mental masturbation . . . as if by touching and looking at these relics they could claim some kinship with the ones who had actually worn and used the items. Their attitude had been not dissimilar from the motorcycle gangs who wore the swastikas and emblems of Nazi Germany—the iron crosses and German helmets—and somehow felt that owning and wearing such items imparted the strength and ability to inflict their will on others through terror.

Yet Goldman, too, felt a strange fascination

emanating from the exhibits. The artistic level achieved in many of the items was astounding in its detail work. One item particularly arrested Goldman: a feathered shield of cobalt blue feathers with the emblem of the Jaguar god superimposed in tiny gold feathers. It must have taken over a thousand birds to make this one shield for some unknown noble.

Representations of the gods of the Aztecs stood in their cases, imperturbable, the countenance and dress showing the overwhelming Aztec fascination with death. Most horrible of all was Coatlicue, the mother of the Aztec pantheon. Her image towered over the others by the sheer force of her accouterments. Her dress was made of serpents woven together as if they were reeds. She wore a crown of two snake heads. This was set off by a necklace of chopped-off hands and hearts, while monstrous claws took the place of human feet. She and her children seemed to wait patiently for the time when they could again feed on the living hearts and blood of sacrificial victims. In their time, blood had fed them—and the Aztecs made sure the gods never hungered for long.

One god, a powerful priest-king, was the most powerful figure in their mythology. Quetzalcoatl—and his symbol, the feathered serpent—was honored in almost all of ancient Mexico's panoply of gods. Even the Toltec and the Maya knew of him. The Maya honored him under the name of the Kukulcan and told of his coming.

Perhaps because this god was so different from the others, Goldman lingered before his emblem. The fascination of the museum had gripped him.

Part of his mind told him to hurry toward his appointment. Part held him here, immersed in the aura of the land of the feathered serpent.

The Aztecs had inherited Quetzalcoatl along with several other gods when they conquered the Valley of Mexico and its inhabitants. There, at the ruined city they called "The City of the Gods," Teotihuacán, they had found the great temple of the feathered serpent and of Tlaloc, the rain god. Goldman considered the irony of the Aztec inheritance. Many of their names for the gods, many of their words for daily terms came from a bastardization of the captured people's tongue—and with the words had come a fateful legend—that of the return of Quetzalcoatl. From the conquered people the Aztecs had learned of the great metropolis that had once stood there and how it had fallen to disease and curse when the inhabitants had lost faith with Quetzalcoatl. Their shamans had then foretold that Quetzalcoatl would return in "one reed," which occurred every fifty-two years. And the Aztecs, taking over the calendar of their predecessors from the few remaining survivors, had also taken over not only the legend, but the predicted time of Quetzalcoatl's return "from the sea."

So it was in the year of Our Lord, 1519, on Good Friday—or one reed, as the Aztecs reckoned—that a fair-haired man set foot on the shores of Mexico. Hernan Cortez had arrived with his men, in suits of shining armor, with horses, with weapons of steel. To the Aztec king, Moctezuma, it was the fulfillment of the ancient legends, for the original priest-king had been fair of hair and had come from the sea. The legends had said that he would return in the same manner as his first appearance.

Moctezuma, believing that Cortez really was the returning Quetzalcoatl, waited too long to resist the Spaniards. It was his belief, not his lack of power, that caused his defeat, for when he had ascended to the throne he had ordered 30,000 people sacrificed to celebrate his becoming emperor. There were only several hundred Spaniards, and Moctezuma could have destroyed them easily. The legend's power was fatal; not until Moctezuma's own son, Qualtemoc, ordered his father killed, was the power of the Aztecs used. They promptly drove the Spaniards from the Aztec capital city, Tenochtitlan. Though many Spaniards escaped, not all did, and for the next several weeks the terrible gods of the Aztecs fed on the blood and beating hearts of Europeans.

But the Aztec triumph was short-lived. The gold of Moctezuma was an irresistible lure, and the doom of the proud Aztec nation was inevitable. Greed—coupled with the religious fanaticism of the Spanish Jesuits, those devoted followers of the Inquisition as ordained by the pious Torquemada—conquered. Goldman pondered the paradox of the Jesuits. Here were men who felt themselves to be soldiers of their crucified God, Jesus, and in His name, and in the name of pity and love and mercy, they did not hesitate in their holy duty. In a religious fervor that approached ecstasy they were able to burn thousands of heathen sinners alive at the stake. This was done, of course, in order to save the heathens' immortal souls—to open the way to the glories of heaven for these heathen. By no means did the Jesuits consider their acts to be acts of cruelty. On the contrary, what they did was done from love. *Ironic,* Goldman thought, *that the Spaniards considered themselves so different from the Aztecs.* For, of course, the heathen Indians had sent their sacrificial victims to their gods in order to deliver their prayers. . . .

And while the priests of the gentle Jesus had burned the unredeemed alive, the soldiers of Cortez had raped and looted—and destroyed the remnants of a great people, all in the name of glory: glory and loot for themselves and for the King of Spain. The story was an old one, and a common one, and for a moment Goldman, thinking of it, lost the sense of mystery that had engulfed him in the museum. He turned away from Quetzalcoatl and walked past other relics and art objects, and then he saw the one for whom he had cancelled his day's appointments and had rushed through the packed, horn-honking, morning traffic of Boston.

The man's back was to Goldman, and he was leaning over a glass display case, but there was no mistaking who it was. The back was broad, and the muscles beneath the conservatively cut suit seemed almost ready to burst through.

Making his way past several other display cases and standing slightly behind the man, Goldman started to clear his throat in order to announce his presence, but, before he could, the man at the display case spoke, his voice deep and steady:

"Welcome, Dr. Goldman. It is good of you to come at such short notice." And with that he straightened from the display case and turned to face Goldman.

Goldman was speechless.

The stocky man locked his gray-blue eyes on Goldman and scanned the doctor up and down. "You're looking well, Doctor," he said. "The years have obviously been good to you. I'm glad you were able to come. For some reason we seem to have our lives involved with each other—ever since that night in the Eighth Field Hospital in Nha Trang."

Goldman's mind did a quick retake, an instant replay of that astounding night in the hospital ward, when, after removing a piece of shrapnel from the brain of the man now confronting him, an unbelievable story had unfolded—unbelievable except for the living proof of it, which was a man known then as Sgt. Casey Romain. At least that was what his dogtags and personnel records said he was called. . . .

"Casca," Goldman said. "Is that what I should call you?" He shifted uncomfortably, but the steel-colored eyes of the man he called Casca held an amused glint.

"It's good enough, Doctor. I will answer to that—or to any one of a number of others." Extending his right hand to the doctor, he said easily, "Here. This is for your collection. I should have left it with you when last we met, but after carrying it around in my leg for the last two thousand years I grew kind of attached to it." He dropped into Goldman's palm a shining bronze arrowhead. "You deserve it, Doctor. After all, you're the one who removed it from my leg."

Casca smiled and looked the doctor over carefully. "Yes, you are looking prosperous. The hair is a little thinner, and the extra pounds look good on you. In Nam you had that half-starved look that people who have either religious or work fetishes get—along with hot eyes and thin bodies. But, yes, now you do look well." Abruptly he took the doctor's elbow with a grip that had the feel of cold steel in it and directed Goldman's attention to the object in the case over which he had been bending when Goldman arrived. The object, the case placard said, was one of the rarest and most priceless of its kind, one of the prizes the museum was able to get the Mexican government to lend for this exhibit.

Casca pointed at the object.

"Beautiful, isn't it?"

It was beautiful, this life mask of deep sea green Mexican jade, full human size, looking as though it had been worn by a living man only yesterday. The workmanship, the artistry, was superb; the mask was detailed to the last degree. The only thing out of place were the eyes. They were a peculiar gray-blue turquoise. There was something strange about the mask, and, had Goldman still been in the awed mood that had first overtaken him in the museum, he might have reacted differently. As it was, he was a little puzzled by Casca's interest. He said, impatiently, "Yes, it is beautiful. But it's just a turquoise mask of some ancient king or priest from one of the Mexican empires. Perhaps Toltec. Or even Maya."

Casca smiled, an odd, tolerant—Goldman would have sworn ironic—twist to his lips . . . as though he knew a secret the doctor did not.

"No, Doctor, that is not where the mask is from. It's from the city of Teotihuacán in the Valley of

Mexico—hundreds of years before the Toltecs. There, when the shamans sacrificed special victims on the most holy of days, a mask was made in the likeness of the victim's face, and the victims would wear these masks when they were brought up to the altar on the pyramid and had their hearts cut out with flint or obsidian daggers. The mask was then taken and placed in a shrine along with all the others that were worn on similar occasions. Actually, only seven were ever made, but they were held as holy objects—something like the relics of the saints that the Europeans worshipped and thought had mystic powers." Casca's smile tightened, became even more ironic. "But, look closer at the mask, Doctor. Look closer. What do you see?"

Goldman let his eyes run over the sea green surface of the mask, examining it millimeter by millimeter. At first he was puzzled by Casca's insistence, for he saw nothing unusual.

And then it hit him.

On the left side of the mask, almost invisible, was what appeared to be a thin line where the jade pieces were joined, but on closer inspection, Goldman saw that the thin line was not a break in the jade, but that it had been intentionally carved—to represent a thin hairline scar running from the eye to the corner of the mouth.

Goldman turned back to Casca, and his mouth dropped open in shock.

The same scar was on Casca's living face: the thin hairline scar that left Casca with a permanent smile or grin or—as some called it—leer. The correspondence leaped out at the doctor. He looked quickly back at the mask. The rest of the features fell into place.

"It's you," he said. "That mask is a mask of your face."

Pleased as though he had pulled a practical joke on the doctor, Casca grinned. "Yes, it's me. And how did I get my face on a Teotihuacano sacrificial mask? Look at the mask, Doctor." Casca's voice took on a commanding quality that was not to be disobeyed. Twice before Goldman had heard that tone of voice. "Look at the eyes of the mask, Doctor. The story is there."

Goldman turned back to the mask, and the gray-blue eyes of the sacrificial mask seemed to blaze with an inner fire, forcing his attention upon them, pulling him into their glowing depths. As his consciousness sank into the turquoise flames, Casca's voice accompanied him:

"Remember, Doctor, where I stopped before? I was at the Hold of Helsfjörd, and Lida had died. The year was A.D. 252, by the Christian reckoning. . . ."

TWO

At Lida's death Casca was inconsolable. The deep black grief that settled over him seemed to have only one remedy: the beckoning sea. Ever more frequently, from his stronghold at Helsfjörd, he would sail out his dragon ship, often taking a turn at the oars himself as if by exhausting labor he could rid himself of his pain, but always, always the sea beckoned, the empty sea. The very magnitude of the gray ocean's immensity—and its loneliness—fitted his need, and the waves, slapping the hull, whispered to him over and over, gently urging. . . .

There came this day. . . .

Glam, the gray-bearded and balding giant, turned from the parapets facing the sea and looked at his friend and master, Casca. Forty years they had been together since that time they had met and fought on the banks of the Rhine, and in all those years Glam had remained Casca's man . . . and friend. Now, Glam's still-powerful frame was beginning to bend, and his gnarled hands could no longer wield the great sword with the same vigor they had known in youth. Of late he had suffered from ague, but he was still a man and a Norseman, a Norseman from a line of heroes. He seemed to sense what his master was going to say before Casca spoke.

"Glam, it's time for me to leave."

Glam pondered the face and figure of his master and friend. There were still no lines in Casca's face, and his body was as strong as when they had first fought. Time's ravages had stayed from Casca. The only change was the addition of a few new scars, visible on Casca's body and hands. Glam knew that other man-killing wounds had left their mark under the tunic. But, enough. It was not his affair. Casca was being used by the gods for some purpose. They were always pulling some kind of trick on poor mortals. Still, ever since Casca had kicked his ass by the river he had been firmly convinced that Casca was no mortal man.

"It is as you say, Lord Casca. When?"

Casca was gazing at the distant line where sea and sky met. "Soon," he said softly, "soon, my friend."

That night in the Great Hall, Casca called out to his men. Most had grown up at the Hold. Their fathers had served Casca for years, and they accepted the fact that the Lord of the Hold did not age. As with Glam, who were they to argue with the ways of the gods? Casca was their lord. That was enough. And he had brought victory to the people, and peace and wealth to the area he held in fief.

Now they waited for his words.

"Friends and comrades," Casca spoke, "the time has come for me to leave this place. To you, my old friends, I bequeath your lands and homes as your own, with your loyalties to Glam, who will be Lord of the Hold when I leave. To him you will tithe and obey."

Glam rose in protest. "No, lord! Where you go, so go I, as always. I am still strong, and can serve as well as any of these young bucks."

Casca put his hand affectionately on Glam's shoulder. "No, my friend," he said, "you are needed here. I must go the way that my fate dictates. I am going to go a-viking. I will take my longships and sail to the west, out beyond the ice seas, and to the south. The journey may be years in the making, and where or what we will find will call for younger bones than yours. No, my friend, your mind and experience are needed here. To go a-viking I need the seeds of your loins, not you." He turned to the hall, and his voice rose: "Who of the young men wish to sail with me to the ends of the earth? To seas farther than anyone has gone before?" He lifted high his horn of honeyed mead, and his deep voice filled the Great Hall: "Who sails with Casca?"

The hall roared. Waves of cheers threatened to blow out the great fire where the meat was roasting. In the red glow of its flames the faces of the young men shone with eagerness, Casca's challenge rushing to their brains like strong drink. This was their chance. It was the thing of which heroes were made and legends born—to sail to the ends of the seas with the Lord Casca, the Unchanging One. All raised their swords and axes in response. "Casca! Casca! Casca!" they roared over and over.

For the young men the years of peace had been dull. It had been too quiet for them for too long. Casca and his followers had long since made their neighbors aware that it was the better policy to leave the gray-eyed lord alone in his domain. The young warriors wanted their own taste of battle and adventure. Their hearts beat faster as they sang the old songs, the words the poets told, the great legends of the north. Of Beowulf. Of the young Glam Graybeard when he had come to the Hold. Even of the gray-eyed man who led them, still young after all these years and all these battles. Now the chance was theirs to become heroes themselves, so that other poets in other times would sing of their deeds. Glam's only son, Olaf, led the singing.

All that night the hall warmed with their drinking and with the feelings of camaraderie that precede great adventures, but the empty seat beside Casca where Lida had sat served to remind him, alone of all the multitude, that everything ends, yet everything is the same. Once more he must leave. The sight of all those bright young faces of his youthful warriors almost deterred him from the venture. He knew that taking them would mean death for many before their sea road ended. He was tempted to call the voyage off, to refuse to send so many to their deaths. But two hundred years had taught him one thing: Men are what they are, and adventure is the way of the young. If these did not sail with him, why, then, they would go with another. Their fates would be the same in the end. It was not for him to alter the way things were. . . .

The morning smoke rose in dark, twisting tendrils into the cool damp air brought in from the sea. The rich, wet smell of the salt spray freshened Casca's nostrils and brought an awakening to his entire body. Alone, for most of the young warriors had gone to their homes, Casca breathed deep, letting his gray eyes sweep over the panorama in front of him, the protected fjord where his dragon ships lay waiting for their master—and for the wind to breathe life into them and to set their dragon heads out into the unknown. A chill ran up Casca's spine, and he wrapped his muscled forearms over each other seeking a little more warmth. Even as he stood, the wind changed and blew around to the land side, and Casca could smell the coming spring. Only a few more weeks and the snow would start to recede, leaving the earth ready for rebirth. Already the first hardy plants must be beginning their stirring that would eventually force their heads up and out of the still white, but melting cold.

When the spring is here, we sail. . . .

He stood looking at the dragon ships, wondering where they would take him.

When he returned to the Great Hall, the sound of snoring reached him even before he was full into the smoky interior, and he let his gaze stop on the massive form of Glam. The great bear of a man lay face down on the oak table, contentedly slumbering in a wine- and mead-induced stupor, his breath whistling out from between his great mustaches, his hand on his ever-present sword. Grinning, Casca recalled the uses that monstrous piece of steel had been put to. Glam was one hell of a man by anyone's standards, and from that time when the two of them had become comrades, Glam's course had always been true. Well, perhaps a little crooked in spots . . .

The sleeping Glam was part of what soon would be the past, but so was this Great Hall. Casca surveyed its dark interior. Armor, shields, spears, axes —all the paraphernalia of war lay about among the sleeping warriors remaining. On the walls the flags and pennants of their enemies and friends flew, equally honored, for is man not judged by the quality of his enemies more than by those he calls friends?

Deep in thought, Casca looked down at the sleeping Glam.

Come spring, old friend, I think our road will finally end. It's best this way. I have known and cared for you too long to wish to see you die. May you find your last battle and have the Valkyrie carry you to your special Valhalla as you deserve. Die with that oversize meat cleaver in your hand shouting to your heathen gods to carry you off to the hall of Odin and Thor. Sighing deeply, Casca shook his head, the thick cords of his muscles standing out as he tensed, then relaxed. *Even you, old friend, have somewhere to go to rest at your trail's end.* He sighed again. *I would even rejoice to share your Valhalla with you. But you must go, and I must wait.*

A scullery maid waited in the corner near the fire despite the smoke and ashes that settled on her hair. Young and strong like most of the Norse women, she nevertheless possessed a shy quality about her. She was watching Casca walking among his drunk and sleeping warriors. Unconsciously she spit on her fingers and wiped some of the smudge away from her face. Beneath auburn hair, tied back, her crystal blue eyes sparkled. Her body was just now becoming aware of its power and promise. When Casca approached, she arose and stood erect. Back straight, she faced her lord.

"Sir," she said, her voice at first cracking a little in fright at her own audacity, "Sir, may I serve you? Anything you wish from me, my lord?" The last was more of a statement than a question.

Casca froze for a moment. The gentle tones of this girl-woman reached inside him and touched his memory of another voice that had been both girl and woman.

He stepped closer to her and stopped where the light of the fire cast soft red shadows over her face. She stood stock still, trying to control the beginnings of a tremor that quivered in her thighs as a virgin heifer does when first the bull begins to close with her. Taking a rag, Casca swabbed it in water and rubbed the soot off the girl's face. He was surprised at the healthy glow that shone through the clean spot. She held her head erect and looked him straight in the eyes.

"May I serve you, lord?"

The voice was now that of a complete woman. In just a few seconds she had left girlhood behind. The touch of Casca's hand as he stroked her cheek had made her fully aware of her power.

Casca spoke softly, as if not to frighten her: "Go and wash, little one. And then, if you still wish to serve me, come to my room. If not . . ."

She turned and walked away, her step firm and

sure, her hips rolling in a way that only women can manage, inviting and female even when virgin. Casca grinned to himself and thought, *They must be born with the instincts of a she-cat.*

A roaring bellow behind Casca startled him, and his hand went for his blade, but then he recognized the raucous laughter that now filled the hall. He turned to face the now-awake Glam.

"By Thor's great hammer, Mjolnir!" the giant roared joyfully. "It's about time you quit mooning about and took a woman! That little she-bitch has had her eyes on you for weeks. Every time she gets near you her tits tighten up like they were cold." He saw the expression beginning to form on Casca's face, and he raised his hand, palm outward. "Hold, old friend. I mean no disrespect to Lida. I loved her as my own daughter. But she herself would wish you to get over your moaning and start living again."

Glam swallowed a great draft of stale mead and wiped his gray mustache with his forearm. "Go on, you dago dummy, or she'll beat you to your bed. Go and get her!"

At that, Casca let his own laughter come through, and the two friends roared together as only those who share secret thoughts can. They laughed, and with that laughter much of Casca's pain left.

Perhaps the auburn-haired young girl would help even more to leave. The pain might go . . . but the memories stayed. Casca walked to his rooms past the smoking, flickering torches that lit the way down the gray stone walls. The stones always seemed bleaker in winter, but the tapestries portraying the great heroes and legends of old, the tapestries lining a goodly portion of the walls, provided a little color against the hard stone.

Entering his rooms, he could see that the fires had been kept going through the night against the chill damp. Food and wine sat on the table with the marble top, the one that had come from Rome itself. He crossed the room to his bed and noticed a sizable lump in it. The girl.

Glam was right. She did beat me up here. Chuckling under his breath, he stood close to the side of the bed and looked down at her. Her face was rosy and shining from the scrubbing she had just given herself. Her hair was let loose from its braids and lay about her like a cloud. She smelled good. Apparently before she had come up to his room she had taken sweet herbs and rubbed hair and the secret places of her body with them. The old women would have told her to do so.

Casca smiled down at her. "Well, little one, are you sure?"

She nodded her head, afraid to trust her voice.

"So be it." Casca undid his tunic and let his Nordic loose trousers drop, and before she was really sure what happened he was alongside her under the feather-filled covers, his body colder than hers and giving her a shuddering thrill as she felt the hardness of his stomach and legs move against her.

Gently, Casca put his arm around her and pulled her close. She snuggled her face into the crook of his neck and squeaked in small tones, "Be gentle, master, you are the first." Taking her breast into his calloused and rough hand, Casca gently kissed the nipple, sending delicious quivers racing through her.

"Gentle it shall be," he said softly.

And gentle it was . . . until the ending when she begged him to enter her deep and tear her apart with his manhood. The small pain of her torn flesh was as nothing compared to the desire she felt to have him thrust ever deeper in her warmth.

Old Glam was right.

The pain eased. . . .

The weeks until the green of spring would break on them seemed all too short for the work that had to be done. This was to be no ordinary raiding voyage. This was to be a Nordic odyssey. The amount of preparation involved was staggering.

Had it not been that it was Lord Casca leading them, few would have dared to venture forth on such an expedition, but these young men had been raised on tales of their strange and mysterious lord. He had bounced them on his knees when they were children, and he had taught most of them their first use of weapons. From their earliest memories he had been the same: changed perhaps, but never older. The greatest change was that of the sadness that had come when his lady, the daughter of the brutal Ragnar, had died. The sadness . . . and the sense of time running on forever . . .

As children, they had seen him in his armor, with his famed short sword, leading their fathers and their elder brothers out to do battle with those who dared to challenge the right of their lord to his domain and Hold. Many were the nights when they had listened to old Glam tell of his and Casca's adventures when Glam was young . . . how they had found their way to an ancient keep after Ragnar had blinded his own daughter because she said she had eyes for no one but Casca . . . how Casca had taken his terrible revenge on Ragnar . . . and had brought Lida to this spot. Here he had devoted himself to Lida, and all who served and loved both him and her made her days good. All were pledged to one great secret: None told the Lady Lida that her man Casca did not age, that while time turned her hair to silver Casca remained as always. He had grown a beard so that his lady could not feel there were no lines in his face from age. All had kept faith with their strange Lord of the Hold. All knew that anyone who broke faith would face his wrath, a great and terrible wrath, for, as Glam had told them, Casca was as one who had been touched by the gods and was not to be taken lightly. But they also served the Lord Casca and his lady as much out of love and affection as they did out of fear and respect for the strength of Casca's arm. To them, they were part of a living legend, privileged to be part of that legend . . . the legend of Casca the Unchanging.

This morning Casca shaved.

Neither he nor anyone else of his people knew that outside in the cold, men were watching the fort . . .

THREE

The men watching Casca's fort that morning so soon after Lida's death might have thought twice about attacking it had they known of the black grief gripping Casca, or had they known of his prowess with blade and axe. Might have thought twice . . . but perhaps not. They were not ordinary men.

They stood in the cold, the icy wind whipping their beards and mustaches. Big men. Outcasts. The thieves and murderers of a dozen different tribes. Their bodies were clad in furs, and they had the feral look of wolves; wolves they resembled so much in temper and taste that no man, woman, or child was safe from them. Their weapons were ready to drink the blood of any and all they could reach. These men-wolves reveled in their bestiality. Now, as they watched the small fort lying below in the valley, they thought it easy pickings. They had watched long, and knew there were no more than forty men in the Hold. The others, as was the custom of this land, were on their farms with their families waiting for the spring thaw to set the fjord free from the ice, for then they could set sail to fish and trade—and occasionally raid an enemy land.

These men-beasts had been careful to avoid any of the farmhouses. They took no chances of being spotted, of the warning being given so that the villagers could rally to the fort below.

Their leader watched. Big. Singularly repulsive. His teeth were black and worn-down almost to the gums. He suffered constantly from toothache and had been known to bash in the skull of his nearest comrade just for being too close when the worst aching came. His beard was black, streaked with gray. He was not tall for one of his race, but he made up for it in width; his shoulders and hips were almost the same size, and his legs were like tree stumps in their fur wrappings. A hide of bearskin served to keep out the worst of the icy wind, but it failed to cover all the matted, dirty hair and skin beneath.

The reason he had been cast out from his own tribe was that he was so cruel even his own kin could not tolerate him. He had been driven from their camps for killing all the members of his family in a black rage—even the children of his own body. Malgak the Killer, he was named—and he was so in truth. No man had ever stood before his axe and lived to speak of it. This well-used chunk of iron weighed over fifteen pounds, yet its owner handled it as a child would a toy.

Malgak turned from watching the fort and grunted to his men to move back to the rude shelters they had set up. No fires for cooking. They would eat cold meat, most of it raw. Like wolves, they had developed a taste for blood . . . and not only that of animals. . . . With the night they would take the Hold. Two hundred and eleven of them should be more than enough to settle with these farmers and fishermen.

Malgak crawled on his knees into the small skin tent he called home and looked at the slender form of the young girl he had taken captive a week before when they burned out her home and put her family to the sword. Her face was dirty and frightened. She whimpered when he entered and drew back against the tent wall, trying to make herself as small as possible. Her hair had once been blonde and her skin fair, but now she was merely a dirty child, bruised, with matted hair and sores.

Malgak stripped his breeches off and threw her under him, taking the fourteen-year-old girl as he would an animal. He thrust, grunted, and sweated over her, slapping her in a futile attempt to get some response. It did not take him long to finish. He looked at her then, thinking of the women they would have when they took the fort tonight. He no longer needed this one, so he took her small head in his hands and snapped her neck as one would snap the neck of a chicken. Throwing the carcass out the flap of skin that served as a door, he immediately dismissed her from his mind, as though she were nothing.

Satisfying his hunger on a piece of raw horseflesh, he thought again of the fort below and grinned, his black stumps worrying over the tough flesh. They had butchered the last of their horses and pack animals two days before. Their food would be gone tomorrow. But no matter. They would have their fill before dawn.

The rest of his hairy band slept as best they could, wrapped in their fur robes and skins, curling up in knots to get warmth from each other's bodies, in the process exchanging an unknown quantity of lice and fleas. They, too, dreamed of the women and food in the fort. The only clean things about them were their weapons. These showed no signs of mistreatment or rust. They were clean, sparkling, sharp—ready for use. Earlier they had cut down fifty tall pines and trimmed the branches off short, leaving just enough to use as hand and foot grips. These would be their scaling ladders. With fifty of them there would be no way the forty defenders of the small fort below could keep them from scaling the walls and getting inside.

Between the midnight hour and the dawn, when men sleep the deepest and the sentries' eyes are fogged from looking out into the dark, Malgak gathered his men, his human vermin, and they slipped silently close to the walls, first walking, then crawling, the snow and ice sliding inside their furs and leaving cold, clean spots unseen beneath the rags they wore.

Inside the fort, Casca could not sleep. The image of Lida kept returning to haunt him . . . Lida as she was when she was young and beautiful. That was how he saw her, even to the end when she quietly wasted away and fell into the sleep of no return. To him she would always be young.

He checked his sentries, giving an encouraging word and a slap on the back to those who looked too drowsy. He walked the ramparts. The cold wind coming in from the sea had the taste of salt to it and chilled his skin into a red glow. It felt good.

Casca wore only a light cloak and trousers of flax, dyed blue. There was no need for armor this night, only for sword and dagger. His sword hung from a shoulder belt on his right side, in the Roman manner. The dagger was in the wide black leather stomach belt that fastened in the back with straps. He looked out on the darkened countryside. *Old habits die hard,* he thought. Even though there had been no sign of trouble for months, he scanned the blackness, using his eyes as he had been taught; turning his head slightly off-center, he searched the shadows with his side vision, knowing that he would be able to see better with such peripheral sight.

Nothing.

He leaned between the stone crenellations and looked down, letting his eyes sweep the rocky, snow-covered ground and keeping his ears alert for any unusual sound.

What the Hades!?

A muffled thump, barely audible, seemed to flow vaguely out of the dark, and then Casca definitely heard an involuntary, whispered curse. *Someone is out there. . . .* Casca slowly, now more carefully, focused his eyes on every shadow and saw movement. Here one movement, there another. Finally he made out definite figures. *Oh, shit. There's a bunch of them out there. And it looks like they're carrying something to scale the walls with. Probably trimmed trees. . . . How many?* Now that he had spotted the first, his eyes seemed to sharpen tenfold and the figures became clearer. From his height they looked in the dim light and ground fog more like the trolls out of Norse legend than men. He came to a quick decision: *Too many of them to meet on the walls. We'd be spread too thin to cover every approach.*

Casca cursed himself for his carelessness. He had been sunk so deep in self-pity that he had forgotten that others needed his care and attention. Guilt slapped him. He was responsible for this.

Turning swiftly, and half-running, he reached the first of his watch. Vlad the Dark stood as silent as his name, spear relaxed in his grip, but the man's physical attitude spoke of his instant ability to turn into action. Whispering in Vlad's ear, Casca sent him to circle the walls and also to send a runner to the sleeping quarters and quietly rouse the men. They were to put those unable to fight down into the dungeons where they were to bar themselves in until the fight was over. The women and children were to be especially quiet this night. There must be no sound from anyone. They had but minutes before the invaders would begin climbing the walls. They must hurry.

As Casca was securing his people, Malgak and his scabby force had reached the walls. Frost from their breaths made small wispy clouds rise from each bearded face. No sound reached them from the top of the walls to indicate they had been seen. Malgak grinned his black-stumped leer, pleased that they had reached the wall without being noticed. It was better luck than he had counted on. Those toads behind the walls and on the ramparts must be asleep. He motioned silently to his men.

The logs were put into position and raised. The invaders tried to maintain that silence that pervaded all in this night. Even the cold breeze from the sea seemed to add to the crisp sense of silence. They began to climb. Those with swords went first, carrying their blades between their teeth. These were followed by the others with shields and weapons in scabbards or slung by thongs and belts from their backs and waists. Fortune was smiling upon them.

Casca had no time to return to his rooms and don his armor. As he was, he would fight. His men silently went to the positions assigned them and lay quiet, waiting for their lord's word to fight. Until then, silence was the rule. The torches lighting the way down the halls were extinguished. Only in the main room of the Hold were the fires and torches kept burning. The rest of the stone fort was wrapped in cold dark. Glam was in charge of the men in the feast room. Casca had taken Glam's son and Vlad with him, along with Holdbod the Berserker, as a reserve force to the hall leading to the feasting room where Glam and the others waited with swords drawn and battleaxes held ready. Anticipation brought cold drops of sweat to more than one young Viking's brow. Many would soon be experiencing their first true battle. They had practiced often enough, spearing and striking with blunted swords and axes, but there they had stopped short of killing. There would be no stopping this night.

In the hall leading to the sanctuary, the way had been lined with piles of fresh straw to keep the deep chill from giving a man's feet frostbite. A door opened on both ends, leading to the hall and further down to the feasting room. The invaders would have to come this way to reach them. Even the entrance to the dungeons and storage rooms below were in this room. The women and children and the old men could not be reached until the invaders had disposed of those in this room.

They waited.

The only sounds were the soft breathing of the men and the thin rasp of metal against metal. Most of Casca's men had on their helmets, conical steel caps with horns of oxen or wings of birds attached according to the owner's taste. Only a few had any kind of armor to cover the chest. Most wore only tunics of flax or leather, but each had his shield, a round thing of stretched hide with a round steel boss in the center. A dozen archers lined the walkway leading to the upper chambers, bows strung, steel-tipped arrows at the ready.

The first invader on the ramparts was a wiry, quick Marcomanni, one of the fierce German tribes. He held his weapon low and ready for the fight. Making no sound, no alarm, like wraiths in the night, his associates in death joined him until the ramparts were covered. Malgak was the last to climb. He was no fool. If they were to be caught on the logs climbing, he would be sure that the brunt of the defenders' killing fell on someone other than himself. Not a coward, he still valued his own flea-infested hide more than those of his men.

But the lack of opposition puzzled him.

"Where the shit are they? Surely they must have

sentries posted somewhere on the walls."

The word sent to him by others of his band was that there was indeed no sign of life on the walls, that the ramparts had been completely deserted.

Malgak chewed on his mustache, killing one of its inhabitants, a particularly large flea. He spat it out, along with a few of his own hairs. His face took on a slightly confused look. Warily, he slowly scanned all of the fort in sight . . . the courtyard beneath, the storerooms by the main building.

No sign of life. No sound of alarm.

"I like this not," Malgak muttered. "But no matter. We know their numbers. They must be here someplace." Still, he was a little uncertain. He passed the word that there might be a trap and then motioned for his men to leave the wall. They racod down the stone steps. One man hit a patch of slick ice, slipped, and fell to the courtyard below with a dull thump that was accented by his back cracking.

Even this brought no response from the Hold's defenders . . . wherever they were.

The invaders swarmed into the courtyard, ready for bloodletting. Surely, here the defenders must fight . . . but, again, nothing. . . .

Vlad the Dark slipped back from the doorway where he had watched the advance of the invaders. He whispered in Casca's ear. Casca nodded and, in low tones, told him to deliver a message to Glam, waiting in the feasting room. Vlad disappeared. The shadows seemed to swallow him as he went to do his master's bidding.

Glam grunted in amusement as he received Casca's instructions.

Casca had his men spread a container of liquid over the straw floor from end to end.

Laughter reached the ears of the silent invaders. Malgak listened to the boisterous, loud laughter coming from the interior. He could make out slurred speech and boasting. He grinned his death's-head leer. "So, that's it. The bastards are drunk. That's why the walls are deserted." He hoped the defenders had not consumed too much of their master's cellar. He and his men thirsted. They had had no more than a few barrels of thin beer for the last two weeks, beer they had gotten when they burned the girl's home.

He gave the order to attack.

Weapon ready, the Marcomanni led the way into the hall leading to the source of the laughter. The rest followed, crowded shoulder to shoulder in the narrow passage. They moved step by step. Slowly. Closer and closer. A single torch lighted the way down the hall. They smiled to themselves. They would have no problem in disposing of the drunken household. It would be easy.

Swearing under his breath, Malgak moved to the front alongside the Marcomanni. He grunted a command. The invaders prepared to rush inside the room. From here Malgak could make out at least four men slumped over tables in drunken stupor, and another two laughing over their cups while they tore at chunks of beef and washed it down with great mugs of mead. Raising his fifteen-pound axe above his head, Malgak readied himself.

Shouting his tribal battlecry, he rushed into the room followed by the packed body of his men. The apparently sleeping defenders all too quickly awoke and raced to the back of the room. The two drinking did likewise and ran to the walls. Malgak and his men stopped in the center of the room in surprise. Their fur-clad bodies sweating from the night's labors and their eyes wild, they looked like brute animals. They stood thus for only a moment, and then a flight of arrows from the walls reached out for them, striking into unprotected throats and stomachs. The archers' orders were no fancy shooting, just aim for the largest part of the body and put as many out of commission as possible. Feathered barbs pinned a dozen of the invaders before the fact that they were in a trap registered in their minds.

Glam and ten men raced from the entranceway nearest the door through which Malgak and his wolves had entered. Another twenty formed a line in front of the stairs where the invaders would have to come at them a few men at a time. Glam struck out with his great two-handed sword at the nearest of the invaders who were still trying to get into the chamber with their comrades. Three fell with one thrust as Glam made a great sweeping slice that startled the ones behind and froze them in their tracks for a moment. A moment was all Glam needed. With the aid of two Vikings he swung the hall door of stout oak shut in the faces of the invaders, locking them out of the room. When this happened, at the other end Olaf, Glam's son, slammed that door from the outside, locking at least half of Malgak's men packed into the dark and narrow confines of the hall. The invaders beat at the doors with sword and axe. Their first sense that all was not well was quickly confirmed—and true panic set in—when a flickering light dropped from above. The grinning Casca had lit a lamp of seal oil and tossed it burning onto the straw they had recently soaked with oil. Fire raced under the feet of the invaders. Crying, they alternately tried to stamp out the growing flames, and cursed when they burned their feet and tried to avoid it. To no avail. Smoke filled the hall. Choking, tear-starting smoke filled their lungs, taking the place of life-giving air. Casca grinned once more and disappeared through the small doorway and joined Olaf, Vlad, and Holdbod. Swiftly they moved through the passageway to the feasting room where the archers were doing such deadly work. The cries for help from those choking to death in the hall reached deaf ears. None could save them. The flames licked up and set fire to leggings, and then bodies. Many beat their own comrades to death with axes and swords trying to escape the choking smoke and body-searing flames. Smoke works fast. Casca had time to look over the situation below from where he and his men had come out of the passageway. The crying stopped, and the stench of burning hair and flesh reached them. In the hall almost a hundred bodies were piled on top of each other, mouths black, noses groping for air that would never come, those on the bottom charred from the flames, their dead fingers empty of weapons they had dropped when they covered their mouths and tried to expel the thick, oily smoke that filled their lungs and took them to their own individual hells.

Glam held off the invaders with sword and shield until the screaming stopped from behind the door. The archers on the stairs kept their missiles flying and provided cover to take most of Malgak's men off him until his chore had been completed. They also gave the cover necessary for a short rush from the warriors in front to let Glam back in their ranks with the loss of only two men. These were overrun and chopped to pieces by the enraged outcasts. The invaders' disdain for the bow as a coward's and woman's weapon proved costly to them as the slender shafts searched out the tender spots of their bodies and buried themselves up to half their lengths in the fur-clad figures. Less than two minutes had passed since Malgak had entered the room, and already half of his men were either wounded or dead behind the oak doors. Screaming in frustrated passion, he and his horde rushed the defenders on the stairs, trying to tear them from the steps and break through so they could butcher those cowards with the deadly flying barbs.

Casca joined the others, coolly giving orders. He formed his men in sections, one section to fight and then step back, their places to be taken by the next rank. That way, no one had to fight too long before given a break. This was the Roman manner when the legion formed a square. The invaders could only come at them four or five men at a time while those behind, in their rage, helped hinder the effectiveness of their comrades facing Casca's men on the stairs by packing in too close and restricting their ability to move and fight. Indeed, many of their men were already dead, being held up by the press of the men behind them.

Malgak sliced with his great axe and downed two of the defenders, leaving one trailing his intestines behind him as he fell to the floor. The dead

Viking was quickly dismembered and pieces of his body tossed back up the stairs to let the others know the fate that awaited them if they lost. Smoke sliding in under the oak door lay in a cloud over the interior, the gleam from the fireplace casting a red glow over the men locked in the death struggle. Even with Malgak's urging and threats the outcasts could make no progress on the stairs. They had twice almost reached the door leading off from the stairway to the dungeons below, but had been driven back by fierce counterattacks from the young warriors.

The invaders took shelter behind shields and overturned tables and benches, anything that could keep those feathered barbs from their faces and stomachs. They kicked and cursed any latecomers who tried to share their shelters. In desperation Malgak opened the oak door, letting clouds of smoke fill the room as he and some of his men entered the hall of death, rushing inside and stepping on the bodies of the dead. Anything to get away from the deadly barbs.

Casca advanced down to the first steps, dodging a thrown boarspear, knocking it, glancing, off his shield. As he came down he stepped over the bodies of his own slain. The sight of the young faces stilled in death brought a building black rage on him. A hot flash rose from his stomach to his face. His features darkened. *Those bright young men . . . to die at the hands of scum . . .*

Glam knocked away another spear thrown at Casca and stood close. "What now?" he asked, his old eyes bright with the lust for battle. "That was good, barbecuing the devils in the hall, but what now? They still outnumber us by two to one. They can't get up to us, and we can't get behind them."

Casca grunted and pointed with his short sword to the oak doorway. "There," he said to Glam, "their leader, the one with the black teeth." Casca took a deep breath and bellowed, his words echoing around the stone walls: "You in there! The ugly one with no teeth!"

Malgak peeked around the corner, taking a good look at the one who had insulted him, though insults meant nothing to him. He was beyond any sense of honor or pride. He had only the feral instincts of a backstabber to guide him.

"What do you want?" he answered.

Casca laughed, his facial scar turning white. "I want you, little man. I want to feed you to my hogs while you're still alive."

Malgak took a closer look at his antagonist, noting the muscles, the scars. The man was obviously a fighter to be reckoned with. He said nothing.

Casca continued, "Come out to meet me man to man, shit bucket. If you win, my men will let you and your vermin escape back to the cesspools you came from. If you lose, I will still spare your men. Have we an agreement?"

Malgak's face wrinkled as he thought out the offer. *Well, shit, what choice do I have? If we stay boxed up here, those archers will pick us off one at a time. But, if I can kill their leader, perhaps his men will lose heart. Either way, it looks as if I have to face him.* Malgak began to psych himself up. After all, he had never lost a fight, and from the number of scars on the hide of his adversary he must not have done so well in the fights he had had to get carved up so much. *Maybe he's not as tough as I first thought. . . .* He made up his mind and called out:

"Who is it I speak to?"

"Casca," came the reply. "Lord of the Hold. Will you come out and fight, or do I have to burn you out as I did those inside whom you now visit?"

Malgak raised his foot off the face of the man on whom he was standing. The sight of the blackened and charred corpse grinning up at him made up his mind for him.

"Very well, Lord Casca. I agree. If I lose, my men go free. That's all I really care about. If I win, your men must give us food to continue our journey. That's all we really wanted anyway, a little something to eat." Malgak was lying in his teeth, and Casca knew it.

Malgak called the Marcomanni to him and said softly, "I will try to get the one called Casca close to the doorway. When I do, you and the others rush out and kill him. Once he's down, those on the stairs will be without their leader, and we will probably be able to overpower them."

The Marcomanni smiled in agreement. "It will be done." He turned and quickly spread the word that when the leader of the defenders came close they were to rush out on him. Their lives depended on it.

Malgak called out, "Casca, I agree. Tell your men to stop shooting and I will step out."

Casca gave the word and told the outlaws hiding behind the furniture to join their comrades in the hallway, that he could have none behind him. Malgak ordered them to obey, and they quickly rushed into the open doorway, casting fearful glances behind them, expecting to feel arrows in their backs as they ran—which was only natural, as that was what they would have done if the tables had been turned.

Malgak stepped forward, round shield on his left arm, his fifteen-pound battleaxe swinging from a leather thong on his right wrist. The axe was single-bladed, with a stabbing spike on the top. Malgak's face was wreathed in a grimy, wrinkled smile. "I am here," he said.

Casca stepped out. The sight of the wretch gave rise to renewed anger in him. The dirty smile and the black-stumped teeth seemed an obscenity after the clean faces of his own young men.

"Good enough," he said, adjusting the feel of the round, buckler type shield he was using, one smaller than that used by Holdbod. "Come on, ugly one, and I'll give you a lesson." He stepped into the center of the hall and assumed the gladiator position of the Gallic school, shield held low and to the front, body turned to present a small target, sword held low to the side with the point slightly up, his left foot leading.

Malgak came closer, swinging his axe in his hand. "That's very pretty," he said sarcastically. "You look like a dancer."

"It will be the last dance you ever see," Casca rejoined, and struck, first with sword, then shield, then one after another. The whirlwind attack of Casca sent Malgak reeling back in astonishment, frantically trying to cover himself. He had never been assaulted like this before—but then he had never faced one before who had won the wooden sword in the arenas of Imperial Rome, a trained professional gladiator, as Casca had been. Malgak leaped backward over an overturned table to get some space between himself and this madman. Glancing over his shoulder, he tried to see where his men were, how far he would have to move to gain the safety of their numbers or have them come to his aid. *Too far . . .*

Taking a deep breath, he came back at Casca, the great axe smashing against the lighter buckler. Then the axe whirled again, and Casca was forced back under the weight of the blow. Casca and Malgak locked together, face to face, bodies straining. The sour smell of Malgak's breath seemed to have a carrion stench to it; the raw meat he had eaten was rotting between his teeth. Malgak struck Casca to the ground with a smashing blow from his shield and raised the axe to split his skull. Casca quickly hooked his foot behind the knee of Malgak, and with his other foot striking the front of Malgak's ankle while the one behind came forward, he threw the childkiller back and down. Now Casca rose, his *gladius Iberius*—the famed Roman short sword—flashing as he struck and chopped, trying to beat down the shield guard. But Malgak regained his feet. *Dammit. The son-of-a-bitch may be ugly, but he is as strong as any I have met.* They closed again, sword against axe, shield against buckler. They whirled and fought, sparks leaping from the blades. They cursed and sweated. The red glow of the fire gave each a demonic appearance. They neared the door, and the Marcomanni rushed out to stab Casca in the back. He was aided in this effort by two other men who fell quickly to well-placed arrows. A shout from Glam warned Casca, and he twisted his body around and fairly leaped into the air, turning into a tumbler's type roll and landing back on his feet. The Marcomanni stood there, an embarrassed look on his face. He still looked that way when Casca threw the sword straight into his stomach where it exited about six inches out of his back, severing the spinal cord.

Malgak screamed in glee. His man was defenseless now without his sword. Malgak rushed. Casca knelt, taking his arm out of the buckler. As Malgak raced to him he held the buckler like the discus throwers of Greece and let fly from the kneeling position. The round steel buckler spun through the air and smashed edgewise on Malgak's right shin, breaking the leg clean, leaving a three-inch-deep gash through which bone splinters were clearly visible. But even as Malgak fell he tried to cut Casca down by lunging forward.

Casca was not there.

Malgak pulled himself to his good knee, black teeth showing as he sucked air in. He shouted at Casca:

"Come to me! I can't come to you. Come to me, and let me give you a kiss." He brandished the axe.

"As you wish it," Casca said and moved closer, circling as Malgak did the same, keeping his weapon facing Casca. Fingers spread, bent slightly over from the waist, Casca moved forward. Malgak swung a blow that would have split his target in two, but again Casca was not there. Malgak tried to raise the axe again and could not. Pain from his leg was beginning to blur his vision. Casca seemed to come from nowhere; the smashing blow of his fist into Malgak's face sent the outcast to the floor, the axe falling from his hand, the shield flying across the room. Casca picked up the fallen axe of Malgak and stood over him, holding the weapon close by the head, the long shaft with the leather thong dangling. He grabbed Malgak by his long, greasy hair and twisted the ugly face up to where he could get a good look at him. Cruelty and animal bestiality was all he saw.

Dark, deep hate settled on Casca. His breath came short and rapid. His heart pounded. His face flushed with anger. He said in judgment:

"You and your beasts dare to come here and kill my people, the people of Lida? I know you. I have seen your kind everywhere, from Persia to Britannia. You are killers for no reason but pleasure, so I will not deny you the pleasure of your own death being too slow—but it will still be more merciful than you would have shown us."

Jerking the head, he snapped a sharp kick with his toe into the solar plexus of Malgak. The black-toothed mouth gaped open trying to breathe.

"Here," said Casca, "here is your axe, barbarian. Then you should have it with you always."

With that, Casca drove the leather-thonged end of the axe down into the open mouth. Malgak choked as the handle was forced past his esophagus. His thoracic muscles moved in spasmodic involuntary actions trying to do the impossible and regurgitate the wooden shaft back up out of his throat. Casca pushed deeper, holding the axe in and twisting. Malgak's face turned as black as his teeth, and he died without the death rattle.

The handle of the axe was so snug that not even his death breath could escape. He died eyes wide, unbelieving.

His men witnessed the death of their leader and slammed the oak door shut, bolting it from the inside. They wanted no more.

Casca rose from the body of Malgak and turned to where Glam had come near him.

"Get him and his filth out of Lida's home," he said.

Weary, drained emotionally by the fight, he walked up the stairs, not noticing the looks given him by his young warriors. Old Glam was right; the Lord of the Keep was not as other men—he was more.

Glam carried out his lord's orders. Taking a page from the scene that had transpired earlier, Glam had more containers of oil thrown into the hallway from the upper ramp. To help the fire along he had more armfuls of straw thrown in. It was soon over. When the first gray light of the new day rose, the warriors of Casca carried the bodies of the raiders to the beach where they were taken out in small boats and dumped in the sea to feed the crabs. That some of the raiders might not be quite dead hindered their labors not at all; they just made more bubbles. The next day the young men and warriors from the countryside showed up ready for action. They had found the body of the young child whom Malgak had used so badly and had come ready for battle. Glam ordered the household cleansed and their dead buried. He ordered that none should speak of this day unless the lord first brought up the subject. All was as before. The warmer days were coming.

FOUR

Each day the indicators of the coming spring became more pronounced, and work on the expedition quickened. The young warriors sharpened their weapons, honing the edges ever finer. Old Corio, the shipbuilder whom Casca had brought to his keep, fussed over the two longships that they would take. Like an old hen over her chicks, Corio clucked and scolded, testing every line and seam in the ships he had built for Casca. The ships themselves were a blending of the Roman galleys—less the ram—and the long, shallow draft vessels the local inhabitants used for fishing and commerce. The local vessels used no sails. When Casca had first come to this rockbound coast, he had been quick to realize the value of the sea lanes. The man who could use them more efficiently would prosper, and so would his people. Making use of his many years as a slave on the Roman war galleys, Casca set about to exploit the sea's potential. He bought old

Corio the ship builder from a Tedesci chieftain inland who had no use for a shipbuilder. Between the two of them, Casca and Corio, they had designed this mixture of galley and sailing ship. Their new vessel could slide through the waves as light as a sea nymph.

The way the new design came about was unusual.

Casca had spent many hours on the coast watching his favorite animals at play, the flashing and twisting sea otters. He had noticed how they turned and twisted their bodies to slide more easily through the rough waters. He had remarked to Corio that if a ship could do the same, it would have a much better chance for survival in rough seas. Corio, then not so old, thought on the problem for weeks. Finally he had the answer. He made use of an ingenious system of interlocking planks that, even when they moved and twisted, still remained water tight. They built the vessel. It worked. They named it the *Lida*. Sure enough, on her maiden voyage, the *Lida* slipped like one of the sea otters she was modeled after between the rough ocean troughs and rose swiftly over the peaks of the waves, answering her master's desires quickly and with a feeling of expectancy. *Indeed*, thought Casca, *ships seem to be more alive than anything else man has created*. The wind, humming through the *Lida*'s rigging, appeared to agree with him.

Although Casca's years as an oar slave certainly did not qualify him as a master mariner, they had given him a feeling for what was right in the way a ship moved through different waters. He could tell if there was something wrong in the basic design simply by the way the ship felt and sounded. This instinct, coupled with Corio's years of experience as a shipwright, enabled them to build what would be the prototype of all the Viking longships that wreaked such havoc in the civilized world three hundred years later.

Now, of the three ships built and lying at anchor, the two largest were being made ready for sea. Corio was as rigid in his demands as a Roman decurion. Everything must be as near perfect as he could make it. After all, he knew these young men who would be going out into the unknown waters with the Lord Casca. He had seen them grow up. He had played with them and taught them seamanship. They were like family, and he would send no members of his family out on the deep without making sure that all was in order.

When Casca looked out on the combination of his young men, the ships, and the sea, his pulse quickened in spite of himself. *You'd think that after all these years it would take more than going to sea to excite me,* he thought. *But perhaps that is what keeps me from going mad. And thank whatever powers that be that women still can make my blood boil; the thrill has never grown old for me. The little bitch of a scullery maid was the best thing for me. Put my mind in order and finally got my shit together. So . . . now . . . in two weeks we sail. The ice is breaking up outside the fjord, and soon the sea will be clear. When it is, we sail. Two weeks . . .*

His thoughts turned back to the auburn-haired girl, and he felt a stirring in his groin—and a feeling of being watched. Turning, he looked to the archers' aperture just to his rear and on the second level near where his rooms were. Sure enough, the maid stood there, smiling, her face bright and shining. Since she had become the lord's woman she now had a favored position in the household and took proper advantage of it to see that her appearance was at its best. Casca chuckled and breathed deep, enjoying the feeling in his chest as the muscles stretched and tightened. *Well, why not? There's nothing wrong with a nooner. It'll wake up my appetite. . . .*

As he headed up to her, he thought, *I'll have to do something for her before I leave . . . to reward her and to make sure that the other women of the Hold don't get on her ass after I'm gone. Women are so much damn meaner than men. I'll give her a dowry. That will guarantee a good husband.* Pleased with himself, he continued up to where the girl was already in his bed.

She, too, was pleased with herself.

Glam wandered through the keep like a grouchy old walrus. He strongly resembled the same, barking at everyone who got in his way. Nothing pleased him. The young men did not have proper respect for their elders. They had no real values. All they wanted was to party. No sense of responsibility. Discipline, that was what they needed. Casca was too easy on them. *I'm going to talk to him about that. If they're going to be warriors, they have to learn to take orders and obey.*

Bursting unannounced into Casca's quarters, he got a quick glimpse of his master well-mounted in the saddle.

"By Loki's bloodshot one eye, man," Glam exclaimed, "I said a little roll in the hay with a sweet girl would be good for you; I didn't mean for you to make it your life's work! Now roll your overmuscled carcass off that sweet young thing and come on down to the hall. We need to talk."

Not waiting for an answer, Glam headed for the hall, grumbling to himself that a man Casca's age should know better. But then Casca always was a strange bird . . . even bathed two or three times a week. *Ah, well, there's no accounting for those the gods have touched.*

Casca joined him shortly. The two sat over a bowl of wine, and Casca took the chiding that Glam gave him, acknowledging that he had been too easy on the young men, but that beginning in the morning he would give them some of that good Roman army discipline and whip them into order in double time. They were good men at heart.

The next three weeks—for the spring did not come as quickly as Casca had at first anticipated—Casca gave short order drill that would have delighted the heart of Augustus Caesar. He gave the young men their first real taste of discipline, of obedience to orders at all costs. He taught them that orders were more important than friends and that to disobey an order was the greatest shame and dishonor they could know. Each man must depend on the knowledge that his comrades would respond as ordered. None could break and act independently. Such was the great secret of success of the Roman legions, and Casca made sure that every man in his command understood it perfectly. These men already had the ability to handle weapons. Weapons they had been raised with. But the concept of obedience to whomever was in command was something new. Twice Casca relieved men whom he had put in charge of work details when they failed to enforce their authority and let their friends get away with infractions of the rules the lord laid down. Their punishment was to be denied the right to go on the voyage. They would be left behind. These two examples, more than anything else, reinforced the youngsters' readiness to obey.

By the time the longships were ready to sail the young men were already taking pride in their new discipline and order. And when Casca told them that to disobey on the voyage meant death or abandonment at sea, they understood fully the deadly seriousness of having order. It was an effort, but they managed to constrain their wild Nordic spirits.

Extra sails were stored aboard the two ships, and salt fish and smoked meat packed in Greek type amphorae were stowed carefully belowdecks. Fresh water, dried vegetables—all the supplies and equipment needed for a long voyage were laid in. As of late the tone at the keep had become more somber as the reality of leaving took the last feelings of childhood from many of the teen-aged Norsemen.

In their homes, the night before the sailing, wassail was sung and farewells made and gifts given. The parents knew that some of those sailing would never return, but like all parents they hoped and prayed to their gods that their own sons would be among those who sailed back to the fjord with the stories and spoils of the voyage.

The time had come.

In the morning they would sail.

That night Casca made his farewell to the auburn-haired girl and gave her a large enough dowry to wed a baron if she wished—or to make her independent, if that was what she wanted.

Glam, though, was something else.

The old warrior sat in his cups, despondent because he was being left behind. Casca took him by the arm and ran the others out of the hall with the words that they would need their sleep. Alone with Glam, he said:

"Glam, old friend, listen to me. We have gone on a long road together, but the time is here for us to part, not because I wish it, but because that is the way of it. I need you here to keep things safe for me until I return. It may be years or even decades before I come back, so it is for you to see that I am not forgotten. Sometime in the future I may need the Hold again, and it is for you to see that my coming back will be welcome. You are my Keeper of the Hold, and when you go to Valhalla, before you go, you must be careful to select one who will honor your charge and keep faith with me. Though I be gone a century or more, he—and each Keeper of the Hold in his turn—must swear to honor my claim and wait for me to return, as I will one day."

Glam raised his red-rimmed eyes to his lord and friend. Snuffling, he said, "I know that what you say is true. I know that I am too old for the sailing you are going on. But my heart goes with you. You have never told me why you are what you are, and I am not even sure of exactly what that is, but you have been friend and brother to me for over forty years, and now with my age I feel more to you as a father would even though you are much older than I. So, my son of the ages, I will keep your Hold in your name and will see that all who follow me do likewise. Someday you may need this place, and it will be here for you. The only request I have is that you take my son Olaf with you."

Raising a horn of honeyed mead, the old barbarian cried out with a voice that rang through the hold:

"Wassail! And farewell, my friend!"

There was one final moment for Casca.

In the early hours before the sailing he sat alone beside the fire he and Lida had shared so often. Lida . . . without her the Hold was an empty shell. Thirty-one years he had lived here with her.

Casca drank deep from a flagon of honeyed mead, his thoughts flowing through his mind. The fire crackled and sparks leaped forth to die untended on the stones.

The road has been long and will, I fear, be much longer yet. But I could not stay here. Everywhere are things that remind me of Lida. Perhaps somewhere out there on the sea I will be released either from my life or my memories.

Memories . . .

They crowd in on me at times. He stared into the flickering fire, made drowsy by the flames, and just before sleep overtook him he set the flagon of mead down on the warm stones. The face of the yellow sage, Shiu Lao Tze, was appearing in the red coals just before his eyes closed. Casca slept.

In his sleep dreams and memories rushed into his brain one after another, appearing and then quickly vanishing to make way for others. At the beginning there was the Jew on the Cross whom he, Casca Rufio Longinus, had struck with the spear . . . and the Jew had condemned him to live until they met again. That life flickered through his brain like the flames in the fire he had just watched . . . the slave years in Greece where he had lived in the mines like a blind mole for over fifty years . . . the Roman arena and the giant Nubian Jubala . . . the detailed scene came back to him of how he had killed the black with his bare hands using the art taught him by the yellow sage from the land of Khitai beyond the Indus River. Casca's own thoughts appeared in his dream: *Shiu Lao Tze always tried to teach me more than I could understand of his beliefs and philosophy. He always said that life is a circle that goes on and on, endlessly repeating itself. All that was will be. Perhaps so. It makes as much sense as anything else I have heard.* . . . When he had killed Jubala he had won the wooden sword from the hands of Gaius Nero himself. It had made him a freeman—for a short time. Then a slave again . . . ship after ship as a galley slave. . . . Then more years. And Neta, the first woman he had loved. How he had to leave her when he saw the worry in her eyes as her hair turned gray and the wrinkles came yet Casca remained the same, unchanging. The legion again. . . . The great battle at the walls of Ctesiphon under the Consul Avidius Cassius—and still Casca was denied death. . . . The distinct image came to him of how he had walked from the legion that day as the city was burning and the inhabitants being marched off to slave pens in Syria. . . . More years whipped by . . . old Glam standing on the banks of the Rhine, daring him to come out. He had. They had marched along together. Then Lida . . . twenty years old and fresh as the spring breeze. She entered his life and heart. Lida was the only one who could not see that he did not change with the years. Casca had loved her to the end, and she was all that had made life bearable. Now she was gone, and he must leave again. The wheel turns. . . .

The images faded from his brain, and in the welcome blankness his soul knew peace.

Casca slept.

FIVE

The longships moved their dragon heads out to the open sea, out beyond the sheltering walls of the fjord, riding up and over the small breakers. The crew chanted in time as they worked the great oars. Not until the ships were in the clear, and the wind blew from landward, would the great red and white striped sails be raised.

Behind, on the rocky beach, Glam and those who stayed watched the ships reach white water.

These were ships designed for the deep water. There were no rowers' benches. Instead, there was a wide ramp on either side from which the rowers would work standing up, twenty men to a side, forty oars worked by half of the eighty men assigned, for there were two watches. Each ship carried a complement of one hundred men. Those not now at the oars either stood on the foredeck looking forward toward the immense sea and thinking of the unknown destination toward which the ship was carrying them or looked back at the receding shore and the figures of their families and friends growing ever tinier. It was mostly the younger men who looked back, thinking of the security of homes left behind, momentarily knowing uneasiness and the quick taste of fear; but the fear soon passed as the greater excitement of the sea reached out to claim them.

Casca stood with the steersman and watched his men as they strove to drive the hundred-and-twenty-foot ship forward. The feel of the ocean breeze was clean and fresh in his face. The slapping of the oars set their rhythm against the slapping of the waves. Then they were clear and in the open sea. The entrance to the fjord was behind, and so was their past. Now for the future.

On Casca's ship the shipmaster shouted: "Set sails!" and as if on cue, as if an echo, across the water from the other ship came the same cry: "Set sails!"

The cloth filled with the wind, red and white stripes brave against the sky. The oars were banked and stowed away against a future need. The wind was with them and drove them forward toward their unknown destination somewhere out on the rim of the world. The sea was open, but a few ice floes were still drifting their uncaring way with the currents.

On the third day they sighted and passed the Orkney Islands to the south of them. To the north was a small group of rocky land masses. Once clear of the Orkneys, they began to bear to the southwest, passing the fabled Isles of the Hebrides. Britain lay unseen in the distance, behind a bank of fog protecting the last of the Druids. Only in Britannia did the Druids hold supreme positions as they had for so many centuries on the mainland when the Celtic tribes had migrated and settled so much of Gaul and Germania.

Onward, ever onward, the dragon ships sailed. Fishlines were always cast out, and brought a welcome respite from salted and pickled pork and beef. Those not on watch or with no duty to perform spent most of their time in the leather bags they had brought for sleeping. These were well-oiled with the renderings from seal and the long-toothed walrus. Water could only seep in at the fastenings. Every small detail had been accounted for, every possible problem anticipated. But what of the impossible problems? They would be sailing past the regions of known waters out into the unknown where all men knew that monsters slept in the deep and would attack even ships of their size and drag them into the murky depths. They had not prepared for monsters. . . .

Olaf at twenty, already over two hundred pounds of muscle, proved himself every bit as capable as his father in the handling of men. Several times in the early days of the voyage he had to prove himself to the others. His quick fists and thumping feet settled all arguments rapidly. Casca would allow no use of blades at sea, but he understood the youthful vigor and temper of men and how they must try each other, so he had no objection to this kind of combat. The process gave his men confidence in each other's capabilities, and what anger there might be in a fracas soon passed with the leagues. They all had a greater foe to contend with . . . the ocean.

Two weeks passed, the wind always carrying them farther and farther southwest. The ice was left behind, and they saw no sight of land, only the endless reaches of the sea.

One by one the dominant Vikings began to make themselves known.

Commanding the other dragon ship was Vlad the Dark. His constant companion was Holdbod the Berserker, a giant of a man with red, flowing mustaches reaching below his chin and a beard that Poseidon might have envied as it flowed with the sea wind. Holdbod had come to the Hold of Casca when forced to leave his own country because of a blood feud. There in his own country he had killed by himself eleven men, all with large families. With the number of blood relatives thus seeking revenge, Holdbod had considered it prudent to flee; while he did consider himself to be one of the best fighters in the world, he was by no means a fool. In the Hold of Casca he had been accepted with the understanding that if he ever let his terrible temper get the best of him there, Casca would personally tear his arms off and stuff them down his throat. After he had seen Casca in action without the use of weapons, Holdbod believed him and gave him due respect. Holdbod was an excellent man with a blade. Only Vlad came close to him in ability in that respect, and the two seeming opposites perhaps found that between them they made a more complete man, for each had something that the other lacked. Casca was satisfied that the choice of the two to command the other dragon ship was a good one. As for his own ship, the *Lida*, Olaf was second in command.

The empty sea stretched before them. For four weeks they saw no sight of land though land there may have been over one of the distant horizons for twice they saw birds they knew nested on shore. But how far these might have flown they had no way of telling.

One day flowed into another.

And then the unchanging pattern was abruptly broken.

On this particular afternoon Casca sat alone, watching the signs of approaching weather. The clouds were growing dark on the horizon. The swells were building. The ship rose to the crest of a wave, then plunged down into the trough. He watched the cycle repeat itself several times. With each rise and plunge of the ship it was obvious the waves were increasing in height. But the ship rode well. Corio had built superbly and both dragon ships responded like well-trained horses to their masters' hands. Up to now the voyage had been uneventful, and the two ships had no difficulty in keeping in formation. By day, of course, there was no problem. They had solved the problem of becoming separated in the night at the very beginning of the voyage by running strong lines between the two ships before dark.

But this evening Casca could smell the coming storm, and his foresight was shared by several of the crewmembers who had made their livelihood from the waters of their homelands. The storm struck just before midnight, racing out of the north, still with the feel of the ice from the place where it was born. It drove the ships forward. All hands took cover except for those needed to man the tiller and bail out with leather buckets the sea water that rushed over the decks. Dark clouds rolled in the sky, boiling and ominous in the flashes of lightning. The thunder as much as the wind seemed about to tear the sails apart with the ferocity of its booming reverberations. It was no momentary storm. For three days and three nights nothing was dry aboard ship. Few of the crew had the strength to eat. Nearly all of the supplies were spoiled from the water, and what drinking water that was left tasted strongly of sea salt.

The wind finally abated. The storm had not been one of the killer storms that could tear a vessel apart, but it had been violent enough to damage the two ships. They needed to be beached and careened for fresh caulking and refurbishing. Also, the expedition had—at most—food for another four days only. Then all would be gone.

The morning after the storm was bright and clear. The wind was gentle as a maiden's whisper. All but the two men kept at each long-oared tiller were sleeping the sleep of the exhausted when the cry of *Land!* jerked them back into awareness. They turned their salt-encrusted faces out to where the lookouts were pointing. There on the horizon, rising dark from the sea, was a land mass.

Casca gave the order to take down the sails and ship oars.

Closer the rocky coast came until pine trees like those they had left at home were clearly visible. But there was no apparent harbor. For a time the two ships searched their way around the coast until Casca pointed out a likely landing at a spot whose smooth beaches indicated calm water. There were forests nearby, so game could probably be found. The dragon ships inched their way in against the tide, bit by bit, the men putting in a backbreaking day of labor on the oars. But finally the job was done and the anchors let down. They had been five weeks at sea without a landfall, but Casca would not let a single man go ashore until weapons were cleaned and ready for action. Blades were shiny, axes sharp, and the bowmen took from waterproof bags made of seal bladders the strings for their deadly bows. Quickly they strung their weapons and refletched such arrows as needed care. At last all was to Casca's liking.

He sent a party to reconnoiter the landing site. The men piled into the coracles of animal hides, made their way to shore, beached the coracles, and then their horned and furred figures disappeared into the forest. Casca thought they were taking their own sweet time, and he was about at the point of doing something about it when they finally reappeared on the sandy beach and waved to the others to come ashore. So another party was launched from each ship, and this time Casca himself went ashore. The unexpected feel of the unmoving land beneath his feet gave him a quick sense of nausea, but the queasiness soon passed when he saw that his men were carrying a good-sized buck deer that one of the bowmen had shot.

Olaf, the leader of that particular party, fairly beamed.

"Lord, it is a rich land. There is food a-plenty, and more deer than in the forests at home. Also large birds. There are signs that there are plenty of bears. We shall not starve in this land, wherever it is."

"What of men?" Casca asked. "Did you find any signs of men in this place?"

Olaf nodded in the negative, his horned head bobbing. "No, my lord, there was no sign. But we have not seen much of the land. It appears that this is no small island but a large land going on for leagues. I climbed a tall tree on the highest hill and looked as far as I could see. There was naught but great valleys and forests."

"Good," grunted Casca in his familiar manner. "Then here we shall work on our ships and make them ready for sea again. But I still want scouting parties out night and day, and a particularly careful watch at night. We shall not be taken by surprise by anyone. If there are people here, then we will be prepared for them. One thing I learned in the legion was to always prepare an armed camp before doing anything else. Get the men ashore except for a skeleton crew on each ship. First we will build here a fort from which we can be secure. Then—and then only—will we fix the ships."

Olaf saluted as he had seen his father do, thumping his hand to his chest. "Aye, lord. So it shall be." Turning, he gave the orders necessary to carry out Casca's will. The Vikings set to work. Axes that carve a man can also cut trees; by nightfall they had built a small, tight camp and were secure. Four more deer were roasting over the fires, sending the rich smell of the cooking venison into the air. Many of the men could not wait and wolfed down large chunks of the almost raw, smoking meat, wiping the deer grease on their beards and mustaches.

But their weapons were always close at hand. . . .

On the following days they expanded the camp, dug trenches about it, and implanted sharp stakes, points out, in the trenches. They added two small watchtowers. Then—and only then—did they beach the ships and proceed with the work of making them seaworthy again. They caulked and sealed every leaking seam, packing and tamping in the punk. They scraped off the barnacles that had accumulated; the ships would be faster when they returned to the sea. They went over every inch of the hulls and the insides of the ships. Corio had built well; there was only minor repair work to be done —and plenty of timber available for it. They worked in relays. While some labored on the ships others hunted and fished. The game was abundant; the waters incredibly rich. The men scouted ever farther inland. Still they found no sight of any salt sea. There were only great rivers and great valleys. They turned their hands to reprovisioning the ships. Meat was packed and salted down, or hung in thin strips to dry in the smoke of their fires and then packed carefully. Birds of many kinds added to the food store. Fresh water was everywhere. It would have been an ideal place to live if they had had women and children, but having none they began to tire of this pleasant land. The urge to sail was upon them. Their confidence restored by the weeks of good food and weather, they looked forward to the time when Casca would give the orders that put them to sea again.

That time seemed long in coming.

During the long days and quiet nights of the

voyage south Casca had had ample time to think. Often his thoughts had been of Rome. He was out of touch with the Empire, for his years in the Hold on the fjord had not brought him much information until he had acquired the services of Corio the shipbuilder who was also fortunately an educated man. From Corio, Casca learned what had transpired in the Empire since he had crossed the Rhine those long years ago. *How long had it been?* he had thought. *Fifty-one years* . . . a lifetime for most men. . . . During those years another stream of so-called "Caesars" had sat on the eagle throne, each having his day and then passing on, leaving the seat of power to yet others. Septimus Severus had sought to restore order after the civil war in which he took the power from the degenerate Commodus, son of Marcus Aurelius. But Septimus Severus had remade the old fatal mistake of giving power to two brothers who hated each other. He had left instructions that after him his two sons would rule jointly, one in the east, the other in the west, from Rome. The result was the old and time-tried result: the elder brother murdered the younger. The year 235 saw the first professional soldier become emperor. When the army took control after killing the emperor Alexander, it installed Maximin. The killing of Alexander had seemed a necessity. He was a coward and a weak ruler, but what the army considered his greatest betrayal of Rome was his buying peace with the Rhineland Germans. To top it all, the peace fiasco had come on the heels of a miserable and disastrous campaign in Persia wherein the defeat was the direct responsibility not only of Alexander's cowardice, but also of his mother's meddling. It was too much for the professional soldiers to bear. They killed Alexander and made Maximin emperor. But they had reckoned without the senate of Rome. That august body thrust Italy into rebellion. The senators won, and they in turn had Maximin killed. Rome saw five emperors within six years. According to Corio the current emperor was one named Philip from the Arabian colonies who had so far been successful in beating off three attacks from Decius who aspired to the purple.

"It never changes," Casca said out loud, waking a sleeping Viking near him.

"What is it, lord ?"

"Nothing," Casca answered. "Go back to sleep. It is nothing of any matter. . . ."

Casca gave the orders.

The ships sailed. In two weeks they saw their first palm trees. The weather had grown warmer every day of the voyage south along this apparently endless coast. They pulled in to rest and stretch their legs along a marshy region. Casca saw animals here that looked exactly like the crocodiles of Egypt, only smaller. They had the same appetites, and Casca almost lost a man to one of them when the fellow bent over to drink. One of the beasts grabbed his arm and tried to pull him under. Fortunately the reptile's appetite was greater than his size. The fellow's comrades dragged him and the beast to shore and dispatched the lizard with spear stabs. They took the teeth to make jewelry.

But they were properly impressed with the beast, for they had never seen its like before. Casca, of course, had. He told his men of the monstrous

Egyptian crocodiles that were worshipped as gods along the Nile. "Some were said to be the length of three tall men or more," he explained. His men looked at him. Three tall men? But no one said anything. After all, the Lord Casca was a most unusual man. If he said a beast was as long as three men, then that was the way it was.

Further south the ships rounded a peninsula, always keeping the coastline in sight. They never lacked for food. A few hours stop and they could catch enough fish to feed twice their number. In addition, there were huge crabs, and oysters a foot across. Ashore there was plenty of game, and animals new to them. One animal that scared the crap out of them, the one they came to fear more than any other, was the snake with the beads on its tail, which it would shake at a man before biting. One Viking found to his regret that the bite was fatal. It took two days for him to die. After that the Norsemen gave these snakes a wide berth.

They continued sailing along the coast. There seemed no end to this great land. Day followed day, and they sailed on. The sun beating on them turned their skins first red and flushed, and then slowly dark. They discovered that after their skins had darkened they could work all day in the burning heat and feel no discomfort. Their furs they had long since stowed in the leather sleeping bags. Now the nights were warm enough for them to sleep naked on the deck.

Two more weeks passed, and they had to put in again for repairs, more warily this time, for they had seen fires at night—not forest fires or brush burnings, but the controlled glows that meant men were on that shore. What kind of men the Norsemen did not know, but there were people here. Sometime they must meet.

When the time came to go in for a landing, Casca stood in the bow, naked except for his loincloth. His hide was tanned brown, the many scars on his body, being slightly paler, standing out like criss-crossed hairs and ropes. He pointed the way in to a good harbor. They had seen no fires for four days, and had laid off this position for two of those days. When they were convinced that there was no one else in the vicinity except themselves, they went in —but they followed the same precautions as at every landing before: First a stockade and ditch; then the ships brought in. The precautions seemed useless. They had seen nothing. . . .

But they, themselves, had been seen.

Eyes had watched them from the forest, the eyes of men. These watchers wore the skins of an animal resembling the leopard, and, like the beast, they wore its likeness in a fantastic headdress, a headdress that made it seem as if the man's head had been swallowed by one of the cats and the man was looking out the open jaws.

These men dispatched runners to tell their leaders of Casca and his ships, and while they waited for word from their leaders, they watched the strange Norsemen.

Had the Norsemen seen them they would have seen men who were as a race handsome, swarthy, square-faced with brown or black eyes. Their bodies were lean, with no trace of fat. These men were hunters. Not of animals. Hunters of men.

They watched the strangers from the sea, puzzled by the huge ships. Careful to keep from being seen themselves, they moved through the jungles of the coast like shadows. The only metal they had was of gold, worn in necklaces and bracelets that were studded with stones of many colors. These were the soldiers of the Jaguar, proud and cruel. Many had teeth filed to points to show their bravery and devotion, to show that they sought to imitate their god in all things.

They were part of a raiding party. They had been sent out to punish a city, a city delinquent in its tribute to their own city far in the interior, near the great marshes in the Valley of the Serpent. Now they watched Casca and his men and waited for orders.

For twelve days they watched, and then runners came back with word that the king and priests wished them to bring back one man from these invaders to be questioned to see if he was worthy of being a messenger. To aid them in the venture of securing one of the invaders' men, along with the runners came another forty Jaguar soldiers armed with spears having flint tips, with axes faced with glasslike rock. The soldiers' faces were painted for war.

They waited.

The strangers they watched were cautious, and the look of them said they were fighters—but so were the Jaguar men.

They watched.

And they selected their man, the one they would take back as a messenger—the big one with the twisted muscled arms and many scars. He was apparently the leader. He was the one they would have.

To attack the fort would be foolish. If they were patient, time would present them with the object of their desires. In the meantime the raiding party punished the offending village by burning it to the ground and taking all the young men as slaves. When they had their last man, they put all the captives in a slave coffle and waited in the jungle for the other Jaguar men to capture the "messenger"—Casca. The captured slaves were bound with ropes of woven leather for the journey to the capital of the Jaguar men, the great city of Teotah. These men were the Teotec.

Now, all that remained was to capture Casca. The Jaguar men were patient. . . .

The time came—as they knew it would. The pale strangers decided the area was uninhabited and began to venture forth in small parties, hunting and exploring. The watchers in the trees made sure that the strangers retained the delusion of an uninhabited land. No sign of the watchers did the Vikings see at any time, even though many of them passed so close to Jaguar soldiers that they might have reached out and touched them with their fingertips had they known they were there. The Jaguar men were not interested in them; they waited for the leader.

Finally, Casca came out walking with the Vikings. He wore no armor. It was too hot, and there was no reason he could see why he should load himself with steel and brass that would surely bake him like a fish in this climate. He took only his short sword. He, Olaf, and a man named Ragnar walked out into the jungle, away from the eyes of their shipmates.

Once the wall of the jungle closed on Casca's small party, the Jaguar soldiers began to move. Making the sounds of birds, they gave directions to their comrades that the quarry was near and soon to be had. Slowly they closed in—first from the rear to cut off escape, and then from the sides. They crept forward, sometimes crawling on their bellies like snakes. Slowly, patiently, inch by inch, they tightened the trap on the Vikings. Casca and his two companions knew nothing of what was going on around them. They had not been raised in woods like these. Even if they had, the mottled hide of the hunting cat that the Jaguar men wore was a nearly perfect camouflage from any reasonable distance, and against the bushes and trees they were almost invisible.

To Casca and his companions the walk was a lark. Casca pointed out the monkeys in the trees. He had seen monkeys himself when he was in the East, but the animals were totally strange to the Vikings. They asked Casca if these little people were gnomes or spirits.

"No," Casca laughed, "they are just animals. But they do have some of our traits, I see." He pointed out one amorous little bastard who was hanging by his tail and getting a little off a squealing female of his species.

The Vikings joined in his laughter.

But suddenly Casca froze.

A sense of uneasiness came over him. There was no tangible reason for it, but Casca had been around too long, had known too much danger not to intuitively sense when he was being watched. He felt that eyes were on him right now. Someone was close. Speaking softly, he alerted Olaf and Ragnar to the danger. He drew his sword on the pretext of examining a strange fruit on a tree and cutting it down. The others did likewise, pretending to taste the fruit. At least now their weapons were in their hands. There was no reason to expect an attack, but if one came, they were prepared for it.

And come it did.

Without warning, fifty jaguar skin-clad figures screamed the cry of the hunt and threw themselves from the trees onto their prey. Weird, strange figures they were in their fantastic dress, but the Vikings were of the stuff that they would fight the One-Eyed Loki himself if he gave them just a little in the way of odds.

The Vikings' swords and axes whirled through the air, cutting down one fur-clad brown figure after another. Back to back, they fought their way to a great tree that would protect their rear. They fought—and sliced the oncoming Jaguar soldiers to pieces. The attackers seemed to be more interested in taking them alive than dead, and the Vikings made maximum use of that fact—until a sudden thrust from one of those ugly stone-tipped spears pierced the eye of Ragnar, sending him to Valhalla . . . if the Valkyrie could find this place so far removed from their homeland.

Catching his breath, Casca carved one more Teotec to the waist and told Olaf that he was going to rush them and for Olaf to slip around the tree and head for the camp, that he would return as soon as he was able. He stopped Olaf's protest with a curt: "Obey. Or die." Nodding reluctantly, Olaf did as he was told.

Then Casca gave a great roar that bounced off the trees and sent hundreds of monkeys into a chattering fit. He threw himself on the Teotec warriors, hacking, beating them back, using every trick he had learned in the Roman arena. Like a living whirlwind he sped among them, killing and hacking. But his sword was knocked out of his hand by an obsidian-lined club, numbing his right arm. Though Casca went on to kill three more with his open hand blows, they eventually overcame him, smothering him under the weight of their piled-up bodies.

The odor of those bodies was itself overpowering. *Shit! What in Hades do these people wear for perfume?* he thought, not at the time being familiar with the use of the juice from the glands of the skunk as an aid in warding off avaricious mosquitoes!

Quickly the downed Casca was trussed up like a side of beef, removed from the scene of combat, and taken into the jungle. To the Jaguar men the mission was complete. They had what they wanted. Let the other pale stranger go. He was of no importance. This one would be the best messenger they had ever had—if his courage and fighting skills were any indicators.

Olaf and a rescue party made their way back to the sight of the ambush, but of Casca—or of even wounded or dead enemies—there was no sign. Only puddles of blood, now covered with flies, attested to the violence that had taken place. Under a bush they found Casca's short sword. Olaf stuck it in his belt. After further fruitless searching they returned to their camp. Olaf relayed Casca's order that they were to await his return. For Olaf, it was enough. He would obey—and wait while he had life. So would the others. Here they would wait until the Lord of the Hold, the Walker, returned. As he said, so he would. Of that Olaf had no doubts. Casca was not as other men.

SIX

The magnificently garbed Teotec warriors were preparing for the journey to the interior. On one of the hills facing the beach and ocean they had assembled their captives and Casca. By signs they made it known that if the captives made no trouble they would be well treated. Using their fingers they indicated that it would take ten to twelve days to reach the city that was their destination. Casca was impressed. The warriors were handsome in their elaborate feathered robes and weird headdresses of jaguars and other strange beasts and birds. Professionally, he evaluated them as a military force. There seemed to be at least one dominant group in the unit escorting them. These men wore the emblem and likeness of a leopardlike animal, but one with which he was unfamiliar. Some of the men seemed to be of higher rank than the others. He presumed these to be officers. They wore the elaborate costumes of feathers and skins. The common soldiers, however, wore plaited suits of some kind of fiber. Their shields were mostly of wickerwork, though some shields were of animal hides stretched over a wooden hoop. None carried weapons of metal. He would have thought they had no knowledge of metalworking at all had not a few worn ornaments of gold. The most common weapons were spears and clubs edged with stone. Nowhere was a bow or anything like it to be seen.

He concluded that a well-trained Roman legion would have made short shrift of the lot—but at the moment he did not have access to a Roman legion. The trip began, the captives led by the ropes of woven leather.

Day after day the party made its way deeper into the interior. They passed many villages, and Casca looked curiously at the inhabitants of this strange land. As a rule they were a handsome and ruddy-colored people, with square features and jaws, but with eyes like pieces of obsidian peeking out from beneath black hair cut shoulder length and with bangs.

During the days of their trek, Casca was introduced to many new foods. One was a yellow grain made into large fat cakes, something like those he had known in the East. There was a particularly tasty tuber plant. But the prize of the lot was a hot spice that burned the inside of the mouth like acid. Something the natives called "chile"—as near as he could make out the word. This the natives used every time they cooked. Surprisingly enough, though, after a couple of days of eating the "chiles" regularly, he began to develop a taste for them.

On the trail the party was joined for short periods

by others carrying market items—as Casca decided they do all over the world. There were pelts from the great spotted cat, snakeskins over ten feet long, and birds—thousands of brilliantly colored birds. The whole countryside seemed to have a madness for bird feathers.

The trail led up and up. Casca knew they were climbing and he was puzzled by it. Was this strange land that big that the interior should be so high? They left the tropical regions behind and entered a desert landscape where the vegetation was sparse, but cacti of many kinds flourished. Several times he saw the strange snakes with beads on their tails that they would shake at one if excited. Although Casca already knew it, his captors indicated by signs that the bite of the reptiles was poisonous.

He became aware of a certain ceremony, endlessly repeated.

As the war party and its captives approached a village, a deputation consisting of the village leaders would come out and make obeisance to the leader of the Teotecs and offerings of food and drink would be tendered. Before the party continued on its way many of the inhabitants of the village would come to where the prisoners were, bringing their children. They would smile and bob their heads in what was obvious approval. Several of the bolder souls would come close enough to touch a prisoner on the head and then touch their own, grinning all the while, obviously pleased. Casca surprised them the most, held them the most in awe. His paler skin and sun-streaked hair seemed to fascinate them.

There was some kind of meaning to the repeated

ceremony, but he could not figure out what it was.

The trails they traveled on were well used. Traffic on them was regular, if not heavy. What surprised him was to find that each night, when they stopped on the trail, it would be at already-prepared facilities—permanent facilities. Used as he was to the Roman civilization, he was surprised to find in this strange land an equally elaborate organization—if not the same, at least along the same lines.

As the party crested a hill on the twelfth day, Casca caught his first look at their destination. Shock—and wonder—engulfed him. There in the vast bowl of the plateau below them was a city such as might compare in grandeur and size with many Roman and Greek cities he had seen. Yet it was strange also. It resembled what he imagined had been the cities whose ruins he had seen in Mesopotamia. There were straight streets and broad avenues, temples and pyramids. From this distance the pyramids looked like those fellow soldiers in the legion who had served in Egypt had described to him. The walls of the city flashed with color even at this distance. It had the feel of being filled with low, square buildings; it had the look of being clean—and of being laid out geometrically. Thousands of the inhabitants were visible. At this distance they looked like ants as they went about their business.

The leader of the Teotec pointed proudly to the scene below.

"Teotah!" he exclaimed, then pointed to the sky and repeated, "Teotah."

Teotah . . . Teotec . . . City of the gods. Good enough. At least I should be able to find out what's going to happen here, Casca thought. The plain below was shimmering with the heat of midday. Cacti, those long-leafed spiny plants that reached heights of over six feet, were abundant. There were also fields planted with crops of which Casca knew nothing—but the fields were obviously well cared for and well tended.

The Jaguar leader sent one of his men ahead as a runner, apparently to announce their arrival. The full party continued at a more leisurely pace. Crowds had already gathered to look at the captives as they entered the city from the south along a broad thoroughfare. Casca was able to get a good look at those looking at him. For the most part, the men he saw wore only a loincloth of white or brown, the women a two-piece dress consisting of a skirt and jacket. Many of these were decorated with geometric patterns. They caught Casca's eye because they resembled the designs he had seen in Greece. But other of the designs were a random blending of colors, no order at all, just colors mixed for the pleasure of it. It was obvious which were the married women; they wore their hair in a bun. The young girls wore their hair loose or in braids wrapped around their heads like crowns. As on the trail to this city, many of the natives would come out and touch the prisoners, making hand signs and smiling. Casca couldn't figure what the hell this was all about; it was a repetition of the ritual that had puzzled him on the journey.

Before the party entered the city proper they passed through the outskirts where merchants hawked their wares and vendors sold the crops of the region. Casca noted that workers and farmers were careful to keep their distance from those of the upper classes—at least he thought they were the upper classes since their dress was more elaborate and their manner more authoritative. There were some whom he took to be the nobles of the city for they were carried in sedan chairs not very different from those of Rome.

As they entered the city proper, Casca could see that the walls were painted in a bright, rich coloring the like of which he had never seen elsewhere in his travels, painted with bold murals, but he was hustled along before he could get a really close look at them. The people lined the avenues leading to what was a great square. They were orderly, mannerly. There was none of the hate and vile behavior that he had witnessed in the Roman mob indulging itself when captives were paraded through the streets. These people were quite well mannered, almost docile, and their deference to the Jaguar men was obvious.

But there was something strange about the whole procedure.

Something that did not quite fit.

It was not too long before he found out what it was. . . .

The Jaguar men stood before the great pyramid.

The priests came forth to look at the captives and determine which would have the honor of being the first to carry their prayers and messages to the gods. The native captives obviously knew their fate and were reconciled to it. The eldest priest, in a great feathered rendition of a monstrous serpent in emerald and cobalt blue feathers, selected one of the brown-skinned captives with a quick motion of his wrist. The man began to sob. Casca guessed that something unpleasant was about to happen. Perhaps they had the same thing here as in the Roman arenas where he had fought. The elderly priest spoke quietly and gently to the man and motioned to the top of the pyramid and to the skies. The man gained control of himself and was led away by two guards. The guards' treatment was firm but full of respect.

A chill ran up Casca's spine, a feeling of premonition. . . .

The priests went one by one until they had faced and spoken with each prisoner. The prisoners were then taken and lodged in separate huts.

Then it was Casca's turn.

The old priest, with his escort of lesser holy men, slowly faced this stranger from the sea. Smiling a toothless grin, the old man said in gentle tones, "*Xiteohua tiotec, Chmpe xaoca huacn?*" Then he pointed to himself and said, "*Tezmec.*" He thumped his meager chest and repeated, "*Tezmec.*" Placing his ancient hand over Casca's heart, he thumped the chest and said, "*Chicxa?*"

Casca didn't know what the hell the words themselves meant, but he got the general idea. He nodded as if he understood and said, "I am called Casca."

The old man backed away from him. There was puzzlement in the ancient eyes. "*Chicxa?*" he asked, tentatively.

"Casca. I am Casca."

Disbelief was in the old priest's eyes. He turned quickly to the Jaguar man who had been in charge of the capturing force and fired a stream of rapid questions at him in a staccato voice. One word was repeated so much that Casca could identify it. It sounded like "*quetza.*" *Shit. That must be my name he's trying to say. Must be the way they say Casca.*

But that was the only word he could make out. While the priest and the leader were talking, Casca took a better look at the pyramid. It was a big thing. A series of stairs led to the top. Whatever was up there was not visible from here, but carved all along the steps was a continuous line of serpent heads, flanking the staircase all the way to the top. Casca looked back at the priest.

The Jaguar leader was now on his knees, drawing a picture in the dust. Obviously he was trying to get across to the high priest how the strangers had come to this land and how they were captured, and either drawing a picture in the dust did the job better than words—or maybe there were no words to explain easily in this language what he had seen. He drew what even Casca could tell was a rough sketch of the Viking longships. Then the leader drew a larger sketch of the figureheads on the longships. Then the leader drew a larger sketch of the figureheads on the longships, the dragon heads. At this the old priest became extremely agitated. Looking back and forth between Casca and the sketches, he pressed his questioning of the leader. And again and again the word *quetza* was repeated.

The thing that seemed to excite the old priest the most was the dragon head of the longship. He kept pointing at its rude drawing in the dust.

I don't know what the hell he's getting so worked up about over a piece of carving, Casca thought. *They certainly have plenty of carvings here.* Again he took in the imposing pyramid. In addition to the painted stuccoed facings, much of the structure was heavily decorated with carvings . . . heads of the great serpent . . . and the likeness of another ugly bastard that Casca knew nothing about. Further, the body of a great serpent was intertwined in high relief between carvings of sea shells and snails. Casca raised his eyes higher. He saw that there were six levels to the pyramid, each decreasing in size toward the top. At the very top there was what appeared to be a temple constructed of dark wood. He couldn't see it very well from where he stood, just the upper portion of what appeared to be a temple. If there was anything else up there it was beyond his vision.

Finally the old priest seemed satisfied with the Jaguar leador's story and came back to Casca. He looked him up and down, chattering in approval at what he saw. The scarred, muscular body of the prisoner seemed to please him particularly. He nodded in approval and patted Casca on the shoulder. Then he took a shining dagger of black obsidian from his belt and cut Casca's bonds.

What the hell? Casca thought. But the sudden pain in his wrists caused by the blood flowing in and setting the flesh cramping and on fire took his mind off the odd behavior of these religious bastards. The old priest gave rapid orders to the Jaguar men. Two escorted Casca across the great square and into a building set slightly apart from the others. Guards stood at the doors. Their flint-tipped spears and feathered shields were different from those of the Jaguar men and bore a snake emblem.

Casca noticed a slight reluctance when the Jaguar men turned him over to the Serpent warriors guarding the doors.

Oho . . . a little rivalry between the snakes and the cats. Perhaps to my advantage. . . . As he entered the interior of the building he momentarily lost his vision, coming as he did from the bright glare. As his eyes adjusted to the dark he saw that his new guards were making him welcome with smiles and bobbing heads. They were pointing out the different features of his quarters. There were two rooms and a small latrine. The walls inside were covered with pictographs representing heroes and legends he could not yet decipher—but they did serve to brighten up the room. Over in the corner near the window was a raised benchlike affair on which were several reed mats and a couple of woven blankets. *Bed,* he thought, *that's what I need.* His captors showed him how to cover the windows and made signs to show that food would soon be brought to him.

The guards left him to his own devices and returned to their positions outside the door. There was no other exit. Lying on the pallet, Casca tried to take in all that had happened since his capture. There were questions in his mind, too many to be answered. What of his men and his ships? Were they all right? Would they stay where they were or come looking for him? He considered the latter to be unlikely. They were sea rovers, not jungle fighters. No, they would stay close to their ships and wait for him. But for how long?

The evening was drawing to a close, and long shadows were being cast across the great square. People were beginning to gather around the base of the largest pyramid—not the one with all the snake heads on it, but the other. Group by group the people came until the plaza was filled. The drab white and sand-colored garb of the commoners was broken here and there by the rich spectacle of the feather-clad warriors and nobility; from this distance they resembled giant butterflies on a field of gray. There was a muted murmuring that swelled and then died as if on command. Then came drums and a distant chanting. The people kneeled—all except a line of warriors who appeared out of the mass as if by magic and flanked the broad thoroughfares and sides of the square. Their lance points glittered like gems; their plumed headdresses sparkled with brilliance.

Casca had been around long enough to spot soldiers, and that's what these were. They were proud ones, too. The Jaguar men and Serpent soldiers were most in evidence and held the positions nearest the pyramid. They faced each other on opposite sides of the square, and a separate line of each ran from the thoroughfare to the steps of the pyramid and up the long flight of steps leading to the temple on top.

Many of the warriors had their faces painted in patterns. The designs apparently had some significance, but it eluded Casca. Most of them used only yellow and red to separate their faces at the nose, the upper half being red and the bottom being yellow, with black outlining around the eyes giving them a weird and terrible look as if they were strange beings from the netherworld—or from a nightmare.

The drums began to beat, slowly at first, then building in intensity. From the north Casca could see a procession approaching. Here were the priests. The priests had a look about them that he could spot as easily as he had the look of the warriors. First there were the lesser priests in front, chanting and waving branches. Their faces were painted black. Apparently only the priests used black as a dominant color. The more important priests following, though, seemed to have more liberty in their body painting for they used yellow and red on their faces along with the black.

As the focus of the procession two Jaguar guards held a man by the arms as if helping him along. He was garbed in the most beautiful of feather robes, the colors so brilliant they looked as if the feathers from ten thousand hummingbirds had been taken and woven in a magical manner. On his head he wore a feathered crest set over a helmet that appeared to be the likeness of a serpent. As the procession grew closer, Casca could see that the man was the first of the native prisoners that the old priest had pointed out. The prisoner's eyes were glazed. Casca had seen that same look many times on the faces of religious fanatics, and also on the faces of men who had accepted death and knew it was coming.

Sacrifice . . . they are going to sacrifice. . . . The truth hit Casca like old Thor's hammer. *That's the reason they have been so careful to get us here alive and in good health. They are going to sacrifice all of us to their gods. . . .*

Step by step the procession advanced. The solemnity of the ceremony was impressive in spite of the grisly reason. The priests and the ones leading the man to be sacrificed walked in stately dignity. The crowd knelt, bowing their heads to the ground from their kneeling position. Only the brilliantly garbed soldiers remained erect. The scene was strange, bizarre, but the orderliness of the procession and the controlled behavior of the crowd was in sharp contrast to the religious rituals Casca had witnessed in Europe and Asia Minor.

The procession reached the first steps of the pyramid just as the shadows of the ending day began to grow longer. They started up the pyramid. At each level some of the escorting party would drop off and begin a different chanting. The remainder of the procession would advance to the next level, and again some would drop off and remain there chanting. This continued, level by level, until only the old priest, two guards, two lesser priests, and the victim were left to reach the top of the pyramid. At the moment when they attained the apex the setting sun was directly behind them, and its golden rays cast a radiant halo over the proceedings.

Incense burners were sending wisps of aromatic smoke to the skies as the old priest turned and faced the waiting masses below. His voice could be clearly heard. He talked to his people. There was no shrillness in his words, no feeling of the religious fanatic. Even without understanding those words, Casca knew the man was absolutely sincere in whatever he was saying, and the crowd apparently felt the same way. Oddly, considering the circumstances, at many points the old man's voice became very gentle . . . as if he were talking to children and reminding them of their duties.

Caught in the hypnotic power of the ritual, Casca gazed transfixed at the scene upon the top of the pyramid. Despite the distance between him and the pyramid top he could make out all but the smaller details, could see clearly what was going on.

Finishing his oration, the old priest made mystic signs to the four points of the heavens. The two lesser priests removed the robe and headdress from the sacrificial messenger. Then gently, almost with affection, they drew him back over the altar stone, his chest bare to the heavens. The old priest held up a knife of clear, gold-colored flint. He faced the victim, the messenger, and began to talk to him. Even without knowing the words, Casca had a flash of insight as to what the old priest had in mind. *He's giving the man the prayers of the people to take to their gods. That's the meaning of this.*

The priest stopped. He touched the man on the forehead with his open palm for a moment. Then swiftly the golden blade flashed in the dying sun. In his imagination, Casca knew what came next: redness . . . a pause . . . then a jerking of the blade and the old man held something in his hand, something red and quivering. *It's his heart. He's cut out the man's heart!* Casca grimaced. A shiver ran over him and he could see in his mind's eye the messenger's body trembling, twitching, and then lying still. The priest took the still-beating heart and cast it into the incense fire where it crackled and sizzled. Casca imagined that even at this distance he could catch a whiff of the cooking meat. The crowd stood and cheered . . . happy . . . rejoicing . . . as if it were a holiday. The victim's body was carried back down the steps and put on an altar at the base of the pyramid. People from the crowd began to file by this altar, dipping pieces of cloth into the open chest from which the heart had been cut. Even children timidly touched the dead man's extremities and then ran to their parents—who would nod in approval at their children's act of devotion and faith.

Damn! Casca thought. . . .

Food was brought Casca. The bearer was a girl. She carried a platter of those leathery flat pancakes of yellow meal together with spiced meat.

When she entered Casca's room she had bowed her head in obeisance, not looking up, careful to keep her eyes away from this stranger with the eyes of colored stones and the hair unlike that of any of her people—or of any people she had ever heard of . . . one with light hair that held streaks of gold in it. She moved quietly, with small steps, and laid his food upon his sleeping bench and then knelt, as though waiting for either orders or permission to leave.

Watching the girl closely, Casca tried to make sense of what was going on and what the girl's functions were. Taking her by the chin, he raised her head in order to get a good look at her.

Pretty. Damned pretty. Her hair was long and gathered in the back to hang almost to the small of her back. Her eyes were wide and slightly oval in shape. Her mouth was full. The rich copper tone of her skin reminded him of some of the dancers he had seen from the lands past the Indus.

"Your name, girl. What's your name?"

Holding her firmly by the chin so she could not look away, he forced her eyes to meet his.

"Name," he repeated, thumping himself on the chest. "I am Casca." He touched her gently between the breasts. "You. Your name?" Again he thumped himself in the chest and repeated, "Casca." *What was it the old man said . . . Chicxa? That's it. Chicxa.* Aloud he said, "Chicxa?"

The gentleness with which he spoke seemed to reassure her. Timidly she touched his chest, but jerked her hand back rapidly as if burned. "Quetza?"

"No," Casca said, smiling, "Casca. Casca. I am Casca."

Shyly she nodded. "Casca." Then she touched her own breast. "Metah. Ih mech Metah."

"Good, we've started to talk." Taking her hand, Casca led her to the window from which he had watched the sacrifice. He pointed to the pyramid, then up to the altar, and pantomimed the sacrifice, the killing of the native by the old priest. Then he pointed at his own scarred chest and indicated a knife cut. "Me too," he said.

Metah faced the pyramid, then Casca. She nodded her head up and down and looked into his eyes.

"When, woman? How long until they do me? Tonight? Tomorrow? When?"

She did not understand. Casca pointed to the sinking sun, then made a circle around his head and said, "One day?" He circled his head twice. "Two days?" He pointed back to the sun, then circled his head repeatedly, rapidly. "How many days?"

Metah shook her head and took her own hand and circled above her head many times. Then with an eloquent shrug of her shoulders she made it clear that he was not to be sacrificed soon, but she didn't know how long he had.

The sun sank behind the wooded rim of the valley, and night closed in on them. The coming darkness brought a chill into the room, for these were the highlands and the nights were cold.

The girl stayed. She sat beside his sleeping bench and watched Casca's every move, her eyes luminous. Amused, Casca said, "Good enough. If that's where you want to stay, okay, but I'm going to sleep." Taking one of the blankets, he lay down facing the door, wondering what the next days would bring. He had forgotten the girl until he caught her slight movement out of the corner of his eye and realized she was shivering in the chill air.

"Oh, crap!" He raised the blanket with his arm and motioned for her to climb in bed with him. "No sense you freezing out there, little girl. I won't hurt you. I'm too damned tired to do anything other than crap out, so get your ass in here and get warm."

Metah pulled herself under the blanket, putting her back to this strange man. Her heart beat wildly. What would he do to her? She lay awake for many long hours needlessly, but finally the sound of Casca's snoring and the warmth of his body lulled her to sleep. Like a child she snuggled close to the source of the warmth. Had she been awake, she might have been awed by such intimacy, for the old priest Tezmec had said that this pale stranger was a gift from the gods, that he bore the name of the god Quetza, that he was Casca the Serpent. . . .

For the next few days Metah was the only visitor that Casca had. During this time he made maximum use of her company to learn as much of the Teotec language as possible. By the end of the week he had picked up enough of the tongue to make himself understood for many basic matters. Using the pictograph paintings on the walls of the room, Metah had tried to explain to him the Teotec culture and religion. For obvious reasons the religion was of interest to him, and, when he was permitted to walk around the great square, accompanied by guards and Metah, he discovered something that made that interest in religion even greater.

When they came to the temple with the snake heads she said, pointing to them, "Quetza. Casca."

The old priest dropped by from time to time to see how Casca was getting on. He would sit in the sun on a reed mat in front of the doorway, looking like a kindly grandfather. His wizened face smiled, and he nodded his approval when Casca tried to speak the Teotec tongue. In his mind he thought: *I was right in sending the woman to the stranger. She will teach him more in the time remaining than anyone else could have. It is good that it is so, for we must talk long with the stranger. There are questions that must be answered before he is sent back to the gods. . . .*

SEVEN

Long had Tezmec served the great gods of his people, for when he had been a youth his father had bound him over to the priests. There were two deities that held the interest of Tezmec. One was Tlaloc, for it was Tlaloc who gave the rains, and thus all prosperity from the land came from him, for without his blessings the land would wither and die —and so would the people. Tlaloc was a god of life.

And then there was the Quetza, the strange one who seemed to fill every niche not already occupied in the heavens. He was the Stranger, the one whose Coming would change all, for it was said that one day the Quetza would come to them from the sea riding a giant feathered serpent, which was his symbol. The Quetza represented an enigma, a question mark. No one knew much about him. The other deities were readily understandable in their likes and dislikes; custom had long established their positions in the hierarchy of the Teotec panoply of gods; but there was little knowledge of what the Quetza was like—or where his position was. To some extent, all gods were mysteries, but the Quetza was the mystery of the mysteries. It was all very intriguing to Tezmec.

Great was Tezmec's love for both his people and his gods. He felt that his nation had been favored above all others. Teotah was the city of the gods; the Teotecs the people of the gods—and he, Tezmec, was the servant of both.

He was always patient with the messengers. He would explain to them that they had been honored and were not to fear, for they had been blessed. Even when the messengers would refuse to be enlightened by his words he was still gentle. He would cluck his tongue sympathetically at their ignorance of the honor being shown them. There were times when the messengers threatened to disturb the dignity of the proceedings. Even then Tezmec was kind. He would make use of a compound brought to his people from the far south, a leaf called "coca" that relieved exhaustion and eased pain. Tezmec would mix a blending of these leaves with certain other plants and with the sacred mushroom that grew in the mountains. Once a messenger ate this potion all fear left him and he felt closer to the gods and the promise of paradise that went with them.

This day, Tezmec moved to the side of his modest home, thinking of his conversation with the stranger shortly before. Tezmec's home was no more pretentious than the poorest of his people. He lived like them, for his reward came from his service to them and to the gods. There were no jails or prisons in Teotah, only houses and palaces where the messengers were housed until it was time for them to perform their act of devotion. Those who broke the laws of the Teotec were not imprisoned or made slaves; they were allowed to redeem themselves by becoming messengers, and all their sins were forgiven them by the sacred knife flashing in the sun. Even common citizens and many of the elderly and infirm would voluntarily ask to become messengers, especially when the crops were poor or other disaster threatened. Devotion was taught to all in Teotah from their earliest days. It was too bad that so many of the barbarians did not understand the honors given them when their hearts were cut out, for it was well known that the heart was where the soul was, and when it was burned in the incense the soul rose with the smoke to heaven.

And soon a special soul, a great soul would rise in the smoke of the incense to the gods. Tezmec recalled his conversation that day with Casca.

A period of three months had passed. Now Casca stood before the old priest and asked: "O priest, o tlopan . . . when do you send me to the gods?"

The old man's eyes had sparkled like chips of blackest obsidian, burning in his wrinkled and weathered face.

"Soon," he had answered. "Soon. When the day is at the longest will be the time for you to go to the heavens with the prayers and messages of my people. It is a great honor. It is a very great honor . . ."

Now Tezmec sighed as he moved to a sunnier spot in his own house. His back was aching a little. His years were long, and his bones were old. A naked child crawled up to him. The boy's skin was dirty, but the child was healthy. The mother was filling a jug at the communal fountain. She smiled as she saw her baby crawl into the old man's lap, curl up, and go to sleep as only children can do when they feel safe and loved. Tezmec stroked the hair of the sleeping child and was content.

He chuckled to himself, his face a wreath of happy wrinkles, as he thought of the stranger and how he, Tezmec, had sent the slave girl. A woman softened a man and made him reasonable. Soon he would be able to speak to the stranger from the sea.

When the day was at its longest, four months hence, he would have the great honor of sending the Serpent God's own messenger back to him. The problem was that he might not be able to understand all the stranger would say beforehand, that it might not be interpreted properly. After all, the gods did move in strange and mysterious ways. Mortals were not always able to understand the actions of the gods. It was also not outside the realm of possibility that the gods sometimes amused themselves by playing tricks on their subjects. Logically the stranger from the sea should have a message from the Serpent god, and he, Tezmec, should be able to receive this message before that day four months hence. But, one never knew. . . . Well, enough. He would do the best he could and leave the rest to divine providence.

A sudden feeling of warmth ran down his leg, momentarily startling him. Then he laughed gently—as did the child's mother when she came to get her sleeping baby. The child had wet not only on himself, but also on the Most Sacred High Priest of the Teotec Nation.

Tezmec handed the baby to its mother, careful not to wake the child. Sighing, he grunted as he rose. It was time to visit the palace of the king. The king was only a child, but already he showed a surprising degree of precocity. He would be an honor to his people. Making use of the same fountain as the young mother, Tezmec rinsed his legs off and then made his way to the palace where the future of his people lived in the person of the young priest-king, Cuz-mecli. There he would teach and instruct the boy in his duties. The afternoon sun on his back felt good, and he would rather have dozed in his courtyard as old men do, but duty was duty, and none could claim that Tezmec, High Priest of Teotah, was negligent in his. . . .

Tezmec met with his student and king. Cuz-mecli was twelve years old and bright, his face alert and intelligent. He listened to the words of the aged priest as they explored the problems of the nation. What to do about the Olmecs? Of late they had been making inroads into the lands of the Teotec and setting up their own idols as an insult to the Teotec. Their monstrous idols all bore the same face, that of the Olmec's greatest king, a throwback and a monster of a man who delighted in snapping spines with his bare hands. He was hugely overweight. The Olmec people emulated him; to them obesity was a form of beauty. The Olmecs were dangerous. They were the brains; the subject peoples of their nation provided the muscle and the warriors when needed. Their power was growing. They were a threat to the Teotec and must be watched. . . .

And that brought up another problem. The

boundary disputes with the Toltec kings must be worked out and a confrontation avoided until the Olmec question was settled. Besides, the Toltec were a vital and dynamic people, almost as advanced as the Teotec. They had a fair amount of commerce between them and that could be of more value than subjugation. The Toltec could serve as a buffer zone between the Teotec and other hostile barbarian tribes to the north. Far to the south the Maya lands were of no consequence. Only a trickle of information about them passed to the holy city.

So, for the moment, little action was required. The Olmec question would have to be answered later after the astrologers made their sightings and read the stars for the proper portents and signs.

Then Tezmec brought up the subject of the man from the sea, he who had come on a serpent ship, the man who called himself Casca. The young king was very excited about his city's captive and plied the old priest with question after question concerning the foreigner. How big was he? Were his muscles really as large as the soldiers said ? Was his skin really so pale? And how brave had he been in battle?

Old Tezmec smiled at the young king's eagerness. Boys would be boys . . . even when they were kings.

"Yes, my lord," he said, "the stranger is very strong. There is probably none in our nation to match his strength." *And probably the only one from the other nations who could even come close would be Teypetel,* he thought to himself. Teypetel was the monster king of the Olmecs who had taken for himself the name of the Jaguar god the Olmecs worshipped. He had inherited his forebears' ugliness—flat nose and lips, rounded head and obese body—but underneath the layers of fat were muscles that could rip the arms off most men like a child tearing the wings off a butterfly. Teypetel fancied himself the strongest man on earth.

Tezmec wondered how the one called Casca would fare in a wrestling match with that monster. . . .

EIGHT

The weeks passed rapidly, one day leading to the next. The guards were ever present. They were friendly, but they were alert, and Casca was only allowed so much freedom. Always he was watched. Several times he had made it known that he would like to spar with some of the guards and try out their peculiar weapons, the clubs lined with sharpened stones or flint—and, in some cases, with jade. But his requests were firmly refused. The memory of the stranger's powers in battle were too vividly recalled around the fires and tables of Teotah. There was no way they were going to let him get his hands on a weapon.

Escape was never far from his mind—even when Metah was in his arms. She had finally decided that he was not going to eat her for breakfast. At most he might do a little light nibbling at night when it was not the least bit unpleasant. As for Casca, his natural ability to learn new tongues served him in good stead as he wrestled to wrap his tongue around the strange, twisting language of his captors. But he persevered. And in the end he succeeded.

Tezmec seemed to take a special interest in Casca's learning the language. When he came around he would nod in approval at Casca's continued progress.

Getting information about his men and ships, though, was more difficult for Casca than learning the language. He tried in all the devious ways he could to pick the brains of those he talked to, but he discovered nothing about the dragon ships or their crews.

Actually, if it had not been for the matter of the continuing line of messengers being sent to the gods—and knowing that he was destined to join them—he might have thought of this place as being the nearest thing to a perfect and happy society he had yet seen. The people of Teotah were the most orderly he had ever seen. There was no sign of thievery—or of any of the other typical vices of city life. Here all seemed to be working for some common goal. There were no prisons as such, and only for those destined to be messengers were there any restrictions at all. Even in the case of the messengers, they were treated as privileged persons for whatever time was allotted to them. Tribute flowed into the city, so there was no question of prosperity. The art and sensitivity of the Teotecs was amazing. It resembled nothing Casca had seen elsewhere. The markets were full of food and goods. None seemed to hunger. The yellow grain was the staple of life here, and it was plentiful. The people seemed absolutely devoted to their city, their gods, and their representatives on earth. Even the boy king Cuz-mecli was a paragon of virtue. His father had himself gone as a messenger when drought threatened the land. He had taken the prayers of his people to Tlaloc, and the prayers had been answered. Tlaloc had let loose the life-giving rains, and the earth had prospered. Surely there was no other greater sign of devotion than that the king himself should send his spirit to the heavens. Could less be expected of the people?

Casca grumbled to himself in his usual manner: "Religion and gods. There is no escaping them. Everywhere I go it seems I am pursued by religion and gods."

The high priest, old Tezmec, had carefully explained to Casca how important he was to the people of Teotah, and it showed in the way the people treated him. When they met Casca they honored him and showed deference. If his eyes lit on an object in the marketplace, the owner was honored to give it to him. As for the children, once they lost their fear of this stranger with the great twisting muscles and many scars, many came to touch him for luck.

Casca felt that he had a pretty good chance of getting away and into the mountains surrounding the valley, but from there he couldn't be sure of the way back to his men. So, if he did escape, he felt that it would not be long until he was found and recaptured.

No. This time he would play the hand out. Maybe he could use the curse the Jew had put upon him. There must be a way. . . .

Metah, though, spent many hours instructing

Casca in the religion of her people and the way the gods must be appeased. She told him of Huehueteotl the fire god who lived in the smoking mountain not far away. But always she came back to the Quetza, whose messenger Casca would be.

Finally one night, immediately after the evening sacrifice, Tezmec came to Casca still wearing his ceremonial robes and headdress. He bowed to Casca as he entered. The Roman knew that this was a special sign that something important was to be done or said.

Taking his elaborate headdress off and setting it down carefully on the couch, the old man motioned Metah to leave. Her eyes were wide, and she was clearly a little frightened. But, smiling timidly, she left the two men alone.

Tezmec indicated for Casca to sit on the bench. "You have done well in learning the tongue of my people," he said. "Now it is time for us to speak." He was quiet for a moment, as if marshalling his thoughts, and then he went on: "First, I must ask you what message you have for my people. How best may we serve the gods from whence you came? What is the reason you have been sent to us from the Quetza?"

Casca thought carefully. This could be it.

"Yes, old one," he began, "I do have a message, for, as you know, I came to you on the Feathered Serpent. At first I did not know the reason why I was chosen, but now it is clear. I have come to tell you that no more must die on the altars, that the great god Quetza whose name I carry wishes no more blood to soak the stones of your temples. In me I carry the message of life. I am the embodiment of the Quetza. The needless slaughter must stop."

Tezmec clicked his tongue in the manner of exclamation of his people and shook his head.

"You speak strange words. How is it possible not to send the messengers? How else can the gods know of our needs—and of our gratitude? We must send the still-beating hearts to the heavens because in them is where the soul lives, and in the sacred smoke of the fires the soul is sent most rapidly to the heavens. If we wait until the messenger dies of natural causes, the soul dies in him—or is trapped until the body returns to dust and sets it free. That is too long a time." He looked sadly at Casca, pityingly almost. "No, my son. You have not understood properly, for what you say cannot be correct. If you are right, all we have done and believed in for many ages would all be a lie, and that is impossible." The sadness deepened on his face. "You are mistaken in what you say—but there is yet some hope for us to understand the meaning of your coming. Soon, in less than one cycle of the moon, we shall send you back to the gods. It shall be the greatest offering we can make. You shall carry all our hopes and prayers with you, and then, surely, when we return you the gods will answer our prayers and all the unanswered questions will be made clear. I am disappointed that you cannot give us a message now, but perhaps we are not yet worthy." He sighed and picked up his feathered headdress. "For the time remaining, until your spirit returns to the great Quetza, you shall be treated as if you were he. From this time until the full of the moon you are a god, and all in this land shall do your bidding—as long as it does not conflict with the laws of our gods. Rest now, holy one. You are blessed most among all men."

He turned to leave, but Casca stopped him with a raised hand.

"It is not time to go, old one. The Quetza lives in me. The killing must stop—and will, for I shall not die. I am the Quetza."

Tezmec shook his head. "Be at peace, my son. Many times have I seen messengers have dreams that made them think they were more than they were. But on the great stone, all is the same. One cycle of the moon . . ."

Metah returned as soon as the shaman had left. Casca told of his conversation with Tezmec.

"The next full moon!" she wailed, tears filling her lovely, almost almond-shaped eyes. Between sobs she snuffled, "I know I should be happy for you, lord. Going to the gods is a great thing. But I shall miss you!"

He took her small hand in his.

"Don't worry, little one. I shall be around longer than you would believe. I have no intention of dying on the altar. Your priest may have to change his thinking before we're through. Now, put out the lamp and come here. Show me how you would treat a god."

Casca was in truth a god to the people of Teotah. Nothing was denied him. The best of food and drink, a new palace, slaves for whatever pleasure he might wish—they were all his. And all were eager to please him.

But he had his duties, too. Every day one of the

priests would come and instruct him in whatever messages and prayers the priest wished him to take to the gods. Each was repeated over and over until there was no doubt in the priest's mind that Casca had it all correct.

Two months before the day, a weathered, wizened little man showed himself at Casca's door. Bowing his way in and kneeling before Casca, he said:

"Lord, I am Pletuc. It is for me to make the sacred mask that you will wear on the day of ascendance."

Casca acquiesced, and Pletuc began his labors. Swiftly, efficiently, the little man's quick hands formed a mold in beeswax of Casca's face. From this, he explained to Casca, he would make a plaster likeness, and then from that would carve a spirit mask in sacred jade. To honor the occasion, after the lord's spirit had gone to the gods, the mask would hang in the inner chamber of the temple of the Quetza as an object of worship so that the people would always remember. It would give them something to focus their prayers on. In the great hall were only six masks. Each represented a special happening, a great occurrence such as the ascendance of Mexilte, father of the king Cuz-mecli, when the king Mexilte had asked to be a messenger and the rains came. The Lord Casca was indeed privileged above all men to be given the honor of becoming one of the great heroes of the Teotec.

Casca looked at the old boy.

"Carve away, little man," he said drily, "but I shall hang the mask in the hall with my own hands, for I *am* the Quetza."

Casca's claim to be the embodiment of the Quetza was rapidly becoming popular gossip throughout the Empire. Already thousands upon thousands were making preparations to attend the greatest day in memory. As for Casca's claim, it was not unusual for the gods to give madness to those they had chosen. It was well known that madmen, hunchbacks, and dwarfs were touched by the holy spirits and were not as other men. On the other hand . . .

Casca spent his days in lovemaking with Metah, and was not averse to sampling some of the other willing maids of the city when she was not around. Even though she would make no statement about his messing around with other women, he had caught a look from her a time or two that said in no uncertain terms: If you weren't blessed by the gods your ass would be in big trouble with me.

Tezmec brought the boy king to talk with Casca. The youngster was eager and curious. Crossing the great square, the king and Tezmec acknowledged the obeisances of the people. Two Jaguar guards preceded them, and two more followed. It was the turn of the Jaguar soldiers to stand palace duty.

Which brought up an interesting little matter Casca had learned about on the grapevine—for gossip in Teotah was no different from gossip in Rome.

The priests of the Jaguar faction were surly enough when they were at their best—but they had been even more surly than usual of late. Keeping to themselves, meeting in the small hours of the night, talking in hushed tones (which became louder when anyone from the Serpent clan was near)—they were obviously up to no good.

It had to do with Tezmec.

Since Tezmec had become the teacher of the king the power of the Jaguar faction had been eroded. The people no longer showed proper deference to the Jaguar god—or so it seemed to the Jaguar priests.

But the priest-soldiers of the Jaguar god now had plans that would change all that—thanks to one of their number, Totzin.

Totzin waited his time. Patience was a great ally. Like the Great Cat, they must show patience.

Now as Tezmec and Cuz-mecli crossed the great square, Totzin was watching their progress. Totzin's face was drawn and bitter with the bile of frustrated ambition. To him, the stranger from the sea was just one more example of how the Jaguar faction was being treated. Jaguar soldiers had captured him, and he should have been assigned to them to use as a messenger. But ever more often the sacrifices were being directed to Tlaloc and the Quetza. And the strongest warriors and most beautiful women were being denied the Jaguar priests, for these Tezmec was taking for his gods.

An inner thought caused the bitter face of Totzin to change into something that might have been called a smile. He did not say the words, but they sounded in his brain: *Soon . . . soon. After the solstice all will change. Does not Teypetal, king of the Olmecs, also worship the Jaguar? Soon, old man, soon. . . .* Totzin moved back into the shadows, feeding on his thoughts of vengeance. The time was at hand.

Inside his own temple, Totzin prepared for a special sacrifice, a personal one between him and the Jaguar. Stripping himself naked, he donned the skin of a sacrificed warrior who had fallen into his hands, a warrior of the Toltecs. The warrior had been skinned alive from the head down to the ankles. It had taken the entire night for the skin to be so carefully removed. Only the warrior's hands were still attached, and they had been smoke cured along with the rest of the skin. The problem was as always in how to keep the skin from shrinking and how to keep it supple. Now a novice priest laced the skin from the back and Totzin sat and crossed his legs in front of a stone brazier, the hands of the human skin dangling from where his own clawlike fingers extended out of the almost black cured hide. The curing process always darkened the skin. Totzin mused briefly about how the skin of the foreigner would look on him, how it would fit. In that case they would probably have to let the skin shrink some.

The stone brazier was four feet in diameter. A number of small three-legged urns were placed in a circle around it. Totzin cast incense into the flames. Gouts of multicolored smoke rose—blue, then red. He breathed the fumes. His body in a trancelike state, he chanted the words of the Scroll of the Jaguar. . . .

So, while the priest of Tlaloc and the Quetza talked with Casca, Totzin talked with his god.

He was ready.

The god must be fed.

The girl was brought to him.

Her breasts were not yet full. They were now

mere ripe buds of what they were to be. Her eyes were wide with fear and uncertainty. Naked, she was thrust by the novice priest into the presence of Totzin. She was made to kneel first, then lie down in front of Totzin.

Totzin's teeth grinned eerily from behind the face of the skin he wore. His fingers ran over her expertly, efficiently. He quickly made sure she was virgin. "Good. Good. You are a blessed child," he intoned. "The first lover—and the last—you will know will be the Jaguar. You will be his bride."

She opened her mouth to scream, but no sound issued forth. The novice's hands choked off any attempt at sound. He held her tightly, forcing the breast bones out, tightening the skin and thrusting her nubile breasts toward Totzin. Totzin moved with catlike speed. Careful not to scar the breasts, he sliced deep and removed her heart. It was immediately offered to the gods by way of the flames, and his quick, experienced hands then removed all those things that made her a woman. Breasts and sexual organs were in their turn fed to the hungry flames. The sacrifice was over. Totzin cursed that he must perform his holy duties in private, in a place that people could not see. But when Tezmec denied him proper sacrifices, then he must make them where he could, even away from his own people. Two warriors entered on signal and hauled the carcass of the girl away. That night Totzin and a few privileged officers and priests would be permitted to feed on that which their god did not consume. The Jaguar was an eater of men; it followed therefore that his servants must also feed on the flesh of humans.

• • •

Meanwhile, in the cooler interior of Casca's new palace, Tezmec and the king Cuz-mecli, having entered the doorway unnoticed by Casca, were watching, mystified, a scene strange to them. The stranger from the sea was leaping into the air and throwing his arms every which way, and then freezing into slow motion, his hands and body taking on awkward positions that nevertheless seemed quite natural when done by this strange man. They had unknowingly interrupted Casca just as he was finishing the set of open hand combat exercises taught to him by the great sage Shiu Lao Tze when he and Lao Tze were both slaves on their way to Rome, Shiu to teach at a great house of the Empire, Casca consigned to the arena as a gladiator. It was this art that Casca had used when he won his freedom, surprising the giant Nubian Jubala, and destroying Jubala with his hands and feet after dramatically throwing away his own helmet, shield, and sword and thus appearing helpless before the astonished crowd. Shiu had told Casca that the art of open hand fighting had come from Khitai, from across the great mountains, that it had been developed by a sect of priests who used it as an aid to their powers of concentration.

Casca now caught a glimpse of his two visitors and finished. He took a blanket and began to dry himself. The perspiration had given him an oily sheen. Wiping off the results of his labors, he smiled his crooked grin and said:

"Welcome, young king. I wondered if I would ever get to see you. Old Tezmec must have decided that I was safe enough."

Cuz-mecli overcame his uncertainty. After all, he was the king. He advanced slowly toward Casca, his eyes wide in his face as he tried to count the scars on Casca's overmuscled hide. He lost count, tried again, finally gave up.

Casca smiled as he saw what the boy was trying to do. "Give up, little king," he said. "I have lost count of them myself. There are only a few that I can recall, only those with special meanings." The face of the Greek whore who had left him with the scar running from the corner of his mouth to his left eye passed quickly before him. *Never try to short-change a whore or out-argue an Arab*, he thought briefly. Then he turned his attention back to Tezmec. "Welcome," he said. "Am I due more instruction today, or is this a social call?"

Grinning his gap-toothed smile, Tezmec responded, "It is time for the king to meet you, to see the one who will be the greatest messenger since his father chose the road to heaven himself and saved the people from starving when the rains did not come."

Casca was all formal courtesy.

"Regardless of the reason, I am pleased to meet your majesty."

The young Cuz-mecli's brown eyes sparkled. He could contain his curiosity no longer. "Tectli Quetza," he asked, "what was it that you were doing when we entered?"

Casca chuckled. "Little king," he said, "more years ago than you would believe—or even Tezmec, for that matter—I was taught what you saw me doing by a man from Khitai, a very wise man from a very distant land. Here. I will show you how some of it is done." Casca was not above a little showing off. Besides, a demonstration might be to his advantage. Workmen had earlier left a pile of rocks in a corner of the room they were refurbishing, and now Casca went to these, selected a rock about twenty inches long and ten wide and three inches thick. He put this rock down on a pile of others, in effect forming a stone sawhorse.

Kneeling on one knee, he drew his breath in and let it out slowly between his teeth. He inhaled again, formed his fist, and then with an explosive exhalation sent his hand crashing down and through the rock, leaving it in two separate pieces.

Cuz-mecli stared in amazement, his mouth open.

Three guards rushed in, weapons at the ready, having heard the sound of Casca's exploding "Kiyi!" breath burst out. Tezmec signaled for them to leave, but their leader cast a wary eye on Casca and then on the stone pieces. Finally, mumbling to himself under his breath, he left, shaking his head in confusion.

Cuz-mecli quickly made a sign to ward off evil spirits.

"It's not magic, little king," Casca explained. "You could learn it if you wished, but it would take many moons, many seasons."

Tezmec shook his head. "No, Tectli. You have not that long to remain with us. The day of your ascendance draws near." The brightly painted murals depicting the glory of the gods and the glory of the Teotec nation seemed to add to Tezmec's words from the walls of the palace.

"As you say, priest," Casca said drily. "But enough of this. What can I do for the king?"

"Answer my questions, Tectli Quetza. That is what I wish. Tell me where you came from. Are all of the people there gods? And do they all look as you do? And where did you find the serpent ship on which you came to us to fulfill the legends of our people?"

Raising his hand, Casca stopped the torrent of questions pouring from the mouth of the young king.

"One at a time, my lord. First, I come from across the great water. It is many, many days' sail to reach my land. It would take the same time as it takes for a field to be planted and to grow ripe. That is, if you were not to stop and tarry anywhere.

"And, no, all the people do not look as I do. There are people of many colors—from almost gold to blackest black. There are even many who have the same ruddy complexion as your people.

"And, no, all are not gods—though many have thought that they were." Another quick flash went through Casca's mind, and Gaius Nero's face flickered before his brain.

But at that moment, looking at the young king's face flushed with excitement, out of the corner of his eye Casca caught Tezmec watching him thoughtfully. *Uh..oh,* he thought. *Better play the game.*

He let a slight tone of majesty begin to slip into his voice, as though he had something of importance to impart.

"As for the ship, it came from the great god Quetza, and it was he who guided me to this place. It was not until I learned the use of your tongue, though, that the meaning of my coming was made clear to me and the message the great god Quetza wished delivered made plain for me to speak.

"I am here to give your people a great message—as I have already told the priest Tezmec."

Tezmec raised his wrinkled hand to stop the conversation. He did not want the young king to be confused by Casca's contradictions of what he himself had taught the king.

"Enough talk, Tectli Quetza," he interrupted firmly. "It is time for the king to attend his other duties. We will meet again another time." It was so obvious that he was thinking that they would not meet again until the afterlife that Casca smiled broadly, irritating the old priest as he hustled the young king out of the presence of this stranger with the possibly dangerous words. Tezmec looked back over his shoulder and said testily, "The day comes soon. Prepare yourself and your thoughts. And remember . . . behave with dignity."

Metah devoted the remaining weeks not only teaching Casca all she could of the Teotec culture, but also figuring out ways she could keep the other women away from him. He might be holy to them, but to her the time he had spent with her made him more of a man than a messenger of the gods.

Half a dozen times the maskmaker came for fittings, to check on small details. The mask assumed an eerie quality as the features of Casca's face in the jade became more pronounced. The maskmaker was an artist who would have stood up against the best of the Roman Empire and of the Greeks. The mask was astonishingly Casca, right down to the hairline scar leading from the corner of his eye down to his mouth. It was his face in jade—deep, green jade—jade of almost gemstone quality. Only the empty eyes of the mask seemed lacking in order to give it a life of its own. It was a magnificent creation. Pletuc the carver was evidently proud of his work, and justly so. He said to Casca:

"Tectli, when the day comes for the mask to hang in the hall, it will live. Already I have acquired the finest of turquoise. It is the same color as your eyes. It will match them perfectly. It is even now being prepared, and when the eyes of turquoise are set the mask will live. For all time, people will know of your coming, and of the honor you have done us."

Bowing his way out, the old carver left, leaving Casca to his thoughts.

Each day drew him nearer to the altar.

Metah helped him keep from dwelling on his fate, but, in spite of the growing feelings he was developing for her, each day did in its turn end and bring another—and another. . . .

He could learn nothing of his men and the longships. Even when he bluntly enquired as to them and how they were faring, he was politely but firmly refused information. The fact that none of them showed up in the capital of the Teotecs made him believe that they might still be alive. But were they still waiting on the coast? Would they still be there when the coming grisly affair was finished? If he returned to the coast then, would they have waited for him? How long would they wait—that was the most important thing on his mind.

Except for one other.

In one week he would bare his chest on the altar.

When that time came, how could he keep from losing consciousness?

He must not pass out. The Jew's curse might keep him from dying in the case of wounds great enough to kill other men—but it did not protect him from pain. If the pain were great enough, he would pass out—and certainly the sacrifice pain would be that great. He usually passed out from great pain. How could he prevent it now?

Others went to the stone while he waited his turn.

He noticed something.

It might be a possibility.

Several of them had a glazed look to their eyes and moved with slow, deliberate steps, as though in a trance . . . or drugged. One even stepped on a broken pot shard and laid his foot open to the bone and made no sign of having felt pain at all.

"Why?" Casca asked Metah.

She told him that sometimes the messengers were given a mixture of herbs and mushrooms. The mushrooms gave them visions, but the leaf called coca was used to stop pain. Coca was frequently used by others. It gave strength to the runners who carried the king's edicts from village to village. The runners chewed the bitter leaf to stop exhaustion.

That may be my answer, Casca decided. *If the leaf stops pain, I may be able to retain consciousness during the sacrifice.*

"Metah, can you get some of the leaves for me?"

She turned her dark brown eyes to him, a question in their depths. "I suppose so, my lord. How much do you need?"

"I don't know. How much do the runners take?"

"A small handful will last them for several days."

"Then bring me five handfuls. I may have to do some testing."

Confused, she turned away. "As you wish, Tectli. The priests said you may have anything you wish."

"Cood woman. Then get it for me now."

Metah left—with the left cheek of her firm ass smarting, but not all in pain, from the love tap Casca administered when she turned to leave. . . .

The two dragon ships lay securely beached on the white sand, protected by a stockade that reached around them and down into the water. The barricade had been put in at low tide after the ships had been dragged up as far onto high ground as possible. Olaf Glamson had taken command of his remaining warriors. Eighty-two men lived, and all but four were fit for action. Time and again they had beaten back attacks by hostiles, until finally their fierce prowess had made them more desirable as allies than as enemies. One of the weaker tribes had come to their aid when they were in battle with the Jaguar men. Between them they had smashed the attackers, and the Vikings' new allies had enjoyed the unusual and rare pleasure of seeing how the Jaguar soldiers would behave under the blade of their priests. First one, and then another small tribe allied themselves with the fair-haired strangers from the sea. Several times disgruntled and weary Vikings wished to board their ships and sail for home, for surely the Lord Casca was now dead, or else he would have returned by now. These objections were quickly quelled by a blow from Olaf's fist, or the flat of his blade. Raising his voice after the last incident, he squared his jaw and spoke:

"We serve the Lord of the Keep. My father served him, as did yours. Never did he fail them, and he shall not fail us or we him. Norak, when last we saw the lord as the heathen warriors swarmed over him, did he not cry out for us to wait for him? That he would return?"

Norak voiced his assertion that what was said was correct.

"Then," Olaf continued, "we wait. Remember that Casca is not as other men. He is the Unchanging One. He is the Walker. And though these strange people cut his very heart out of him, I know he will return. He is Casca, Lord of the Keep, and our lord. Who would dare to face his wrath if we left without him and he should come upon us in the future?"

Olaf's crystal blue eyes searched the faces of his warriors for a dissenting answer.

There was none.

"Then we wait. Though it take the time for all of us to become graybeards, we wait."

NINE

The jade mask stifled Casca. It seemed to imprison his brain in a green dungeon. He walked slowly to the beat of the drums. The heat of the day was overpowering. Trickles of sweat ran down Casca's back, and his armpits felt as though they were filled with wet mud. Through the eyeholes in the mask he looked through waves of shimmering air that distorted anything over a hundred feet away. Through the shimmering heat waves the distant pyramid of the Quetza, two miles away, seemed floating above the earth, suspended as in a dream . . . or nightmare.

Step, step, step to the sacrifice. The throbbing of the drums beat in rhythm with his own pulse, step by step, each step a beat of the skin-covered drums. The reed pipes shrilled; the flutes cried. Every sound seemed doubled, repeated, doubled again. He imagined he could hear the beating of his own heart, in monstrous rhythm with the obscene drums. In the shimmering heat waves the brilliant emerald green robe of feathers that covered his shoulders and reached to his knees reflected thousands of pinpoints where the sun hit them.

The great Serpent headdress was amazingly light.

Step. Step. Step. Everything had an endless repetition . . . step, shimmer, beat . . . beat, step, shimmer . . . through the endless crowd that lined the way to the pyramid. As he passed, all would fall and bow their faces before him . . . endlessly repeating. . . .

The taste of the coca distillation was bitter in his mouth. His senses seemed to be far apart from his consciousness . . . as though he were two separate persons, but each a not-quite-complete entity.

Only Tezmec was in front of him; to the side walked an honor guard of lesser priests and soldiers. The heaviness of the day was like nothing he had ever known . . . or had he? That day in Judea had been oppressive, too. The image of that day flickered in his brain, brought back the feelings, the taste, the sight . . . the menacing heaviness of the hot air.

Brrrum, brrum . . . . Over and over the drums pounded their way into his brain. With each beat and step, time assumed a kind of distorted reality, as though time were itself a thing, heavy, dark, and solid.

Then he was there.

The foot of the pyramid.

Chanting broke its way to the forefront of his awareness. When had it begun? It engulfed him in a molten wave of sound. He made the first step up the pyramid. Then another. And another. Focusing his attention on the old high priest's back, he climbed, the chanting growing distant as they neared the top.

The thongs holding the mask to his face felt as if they were cutting into his skin, but the sensation of pain was oddly removed from him. It was as though it were happening to someone else. . . .

They were there.

The top of the pyramid.

The stone, black with the blood of thousands of victims, was before him. The chanting of the priests continued, seeming now to be flowing up the sides of the pyramid and louder here at the top.

At that moment a beginning wind tugged gently at Casca's feathered cloak and caused him to look at the sky. It was even darker, more oppressive than on the long walk. To the west great clouds were gathering, and even from this distance they appeared to be like great cumulus stallions racing through the heavens on some never-ending odyssey that mortal man had no share in. Over the palace, a bank of lightning suddenly flickered. The wind freshened, bringing a smell of salt from the sea.

Storm.

Coming.

Tezmec stood, arms raised to the skies, his old voice growing in strength as he called to his gods to accept this token of their worshippers' devotion and love.

The measured beat of the drums that had never ceased was now echoed by the approaching wall of dark clouds. The first distinct gusts of the rising wind would be whipping around the base of the pyramid, blending with the sudden uneasiness of the hundred thousand waiting worshipers, an uneasiness so strong it seemed to rise with the beat of the drums and be felt here on the top of the pyramid.

Casca looked back to the city below. The eyeholes in the jade mask seemed to take him to the very place; he was seeing it as though he were down there. The great square was a solid mass of humanity in all its varied forms, rich and poor, thin and fat, weak and strong. Every square foot as far as the eye could see was covered with waiting, expectant humanity. Even the rooftops looked as though colonies of ants were covering them.

The first of the dark clouds reached them. Shadows raced across the land. The sky grew still darker. The wind strengthened again.

Storm.

Lightning.

Thunder.

"It's like the day of the Jew, Yeshua," Casca said in the Latin of the Caesars, the Latin of his youth, the Latin of That Day. . . .

Tezmec paused in his oration, the approaching thunder having drowned out some of his words as though the onrushing storm was a sign.

Casca raised his face to the increasing darkness, the wind rustling in the feathers of his brilliant robe and headdress.

The mask seemed to be growing into his face.

Casca felt strange forces pulling at him.

Stop it, Jew! his silent thoughts seemed to scream in his mind. *This is my day. Leave me alone. I am a better man than you, and what I will endure this day is greater than the pain you felt on the Cross.* And then thoughts and words melded, and he was shouting into the wind: "I am Casca, son of Rome, soldier of the legions, and I will beat you! I will endure more than you and triumph. Leave me alone!"

Tezmec touched his shoulder.

"What are you screaming, my son? In what strange tongue do you speak? Please do not spoil this great day with unseemly behavior. Remember your dignity!" His voice cracked as he chastised Casca, "Remember your dignity!"

Casca laughed bitterly. "Dignity, old man? What dignity is there in death like this? Death, when it serves no purpose, is not dignity. It is useless."

Abruptly the darkness was upon them, as if a curtain had been drawn suddenly. A murmur ran through the waiting thousands. The thunder rumbled, and the ground quivered.

Tezmec took the helmet from Casca's head and freed the bindings of the feathered robe.

"It is time, my son. The gods are impatient. The signs and portents of this day are great."

The two lesser priests reached to take Casca by the shoulders and lay him on the altar.

"No!"

Casca pushed them away. "First I must speak." He turned from the stone and faced out to the masses below.

Filling his lungs to fight against the thunder and wind, he cried:

"I am the Quetzu.

"The one whose coming was foretold.

"In this body is the living spirit of the Feathered

Serpent.

"The wish of the Quetza is that there shall be no more sacrifices. With me it ends, and I shall place the mask of jade in the great hall with my own hands, for it is not yet time for me to die."

He turned to Tezmec, and his voice thundered: "Priest of the Teotoc! You cannot take that which is not yours. It is not for mortals to take my life. Only a god can kill a god. But try if you must."

The wind screamed mindlessly. Raindrops, fat and heavy, made puffs of dust jump around the stone upon which so many living hearts had been cut out.

They were like that at the foot of the Cross. . . .

The ground trembled.

Is this my crucifixion?

Ignoring the hands of the priests, Casca lay himself upon the stone. The feel of the well-used granite was cool against his back.

Is it time for me to die?

Are you coming again, Jew?

Is it now that I shall be set free?

The darkness was upon them, and in that darkness Tezmec raised the shining blade of golden flint. The beat of the drums was a distant memory. The knife flashed, and, as it did, lightning burst from the heavens, sending blinding streaks of light breaking through the darkness.

Is it time to set me free?

Pain.

Burning.

Cold.

The shining knife struck deep.

Behind the jade mask Casca bit through his lower lip, his teeth grinding against each other. A coldness like nothing he had ever felt or imagined ran over him.

Is this death? Are you here, Jew?

A greater pain . . . and a tugging deep inside . . . and a sudden feeling of emptiness.

Tezmec held the beating heart of Casca in his hand, blood spurting from the severed aorta. The organ emptied itself on the altar.

Jew, came Casca's unspoken pleading, *now I can die*. The coldness reached to the ends of his fingers and feet, his body chilling in the death spasms. The storm raged, and the darkness was a blanket of black nothingness. The wind screamed as if in some terrible pain of its own.

The people covered their heads and faces. Clearly this was the work of the gods. Tezmec stood, confused, as the wind tried to tear his robes from him.

Lightning reached from the heavens and struck the base of the pyramid, then walked its way up to the altar on which Casca lay, his chest open to the skies. It struck again, enveloping the top of the pyramid and all upon it in a crackling green inferno, the main bolt centering on Casca's body, the electric shocks sending his flesh into uncontrolled fits of jerking. The last remnants of his life force and consciousness asked once more the question: *Jew, can I die now?*

With that terrible voice that had sent Casca upon his wanderings came the words of the crucified Yeshua:

"As you are, so you shall remain."

Lightning flashed continually, the thunder echoing and echoing, reverberating over the land. The wind was as nothing he ever felt.

Tezmec stood frozen.

A burning phosphorescence—like the kind seen at sea that hovers over the masts of ships and travels along the decks—enveloped the sacrificial stone. The jade mask glowed and seemed to throw out rays of emerald light. Tezmec held the still-beating heart in his hand. It was throbbing and moving as if trying to get away, twisting in his grip, slippery and bloody. The golden knife dropped from Tezmec's grasp when another hand covered his.

Casca, his body enveloped in the green fire of the sea, stood holding Tezmec's hand stationary over the altar fire in which the heart was to have been burned. And then Casca took his own beating heart out of the priest's hand.

"I told you I was a god. It takes a god to kill a god, and my time is not yet come."

Tezmec was paralyzed with fear. Then, like a puppet with its strings cut, he fell on his face in front of Casca.

Casca turned to the terrified masses below, his chest cavity agape and bleeding from the ragged, serrated edges of the golden knife. Holding his beating heart in his hand above his head, he cried out:

"Look and see that which none has seen before!"

The multitude trembled as they obeyed, as they watched Casca take his own heart and put it back into his chest.

"I am the Quetza!" he screamed.

He put his hands on either side of his open chest and pushed the edges together, sealing them. His heart back where it belonged, still beating, the terrible pain seemed to be a distant echo. Raising his arms to the raging sky, he cried out in Latin. The rain beat on his face and washed rivulets of blood down through the hairs of his chest and onto his legs, until the life essence of Casca ran red on the floor of the pyramid. Rage filled his words:

"You win again, Jew, and I am what you made of me. I am Casca. I am the Quetza."

His voice rose to compete with and to beat down the screaming of the storm, and in Teotoc he thundered:

"*I am God!*"

TEN

The pain was terrible.

Step by step Casca made his way back down the long flight of steps, past the intertwined carvings of serpents, past the goggle-eyed rain god Tlaloc.

No chanting.

No ceremony.

This time the only sound was that of the storm raging around the temple and the pyramid. The people and the priests were silent. Motionless. Stunned. Less lifelike than the stone carvings.

As though time had stopped for them.

As though they were frozen in a nightmare.

And only Casca moved.

Casca and the storm.

He and the storm were one.

Step by step.

Casca fought away the tremendous pain. Nausea boiled within him as fiercely as the storm without and threatened to throw the insides of his stomach to the raging wind.

Sweat ran freely down from the inside of his mask. His throat constricted and tightened. Mindless of the people about him he moved. The greater the pain the more powerful became his step until he was striding, head erect, a proud image, a god indeed. They bowed. They prostrated themselves before him.

Step by measured step he proceeded past their prone bodies toward his quarters, himself now the full and only embodiment of ceremony, the thundering storm his only escort.

But, although to them he might be a triumphant god riding the wind, to him the effects of the coca leaves were wearing off, the pain was intensifying, and he was beginning to feel the real world around him, conscious now of the rain starting to fall, rain that would be a curtain of water in moments . . . like the curtain of unconsciousness rapidly overtaking him. He had only seconds. He might not reach the safety of his quarters. Yet he knew he must not let them see their god collapse in the mud so near to security. His hands and feet felt numb, distant. The aching throbbing in his chest was all-present, the pain there overshadowing all else. He could not endure. . . .

But in the last few seconds before he was certain the end was upon him he found himself at the doorway of his quarters. Turning, he took the jade mask from his face.

"Hear me!" His voice boomed out with all his remaining strength, one tremendous superhuman sound, for the louder he cried out the more bearable the pain seemed to be. His voice overrode the storm. "Let none disturb me until I next come forth! Only the woman Metah will attend my needs. I repeat: Let none disturb me until I am ready!"

With that final roar, he turned to the interior. But the effort exhausted him. Once in the shadows he barely had strength to make it to the couch. In the very act of falling on the blankets he was unconscious.

The coca leaves had done their job.

Now it was time to heal.

For the next two weeks only Metah dared to enter the quarters of the living god. Chills and fever racked Casca's body. Metah would lie with him, holding herself close against him to give him her warmth to fight off the terrible deathcold enveloping him. She fed him as a mother feeds a child, spoonful by spoonful. Alone in the shadows with him she would cry and kiss tenderly the great wound on his chest. To her he was not a god. He was a man. A man she loved. Everything else was secondary. Even to the priests when they questioned her would she say nothing but that the lord Tectli Casca, sleeps, and when he is ready he will come forth.

Tezmec had a problem. He spent the long days—and even longer nights—questioning himself. He had been shaken to the roots of his being. All the days of his life he had been taught obedience to the gods and their laws. He had thought he knew all. Now. . .

True, Casca, the one from the sea, had performed a miracle.

But all that Casca had done was contradictory to

Tezmec's teachings. And the pale stranger could not be right concerning the command that there be no more messengers.

The gods must have sacrifices.

Inside Casca's body changes were taking place. Millimeter by millimeter his heart was returning to its proper function and position. The severed blood vessels and arteries were repairing the damage, seeking again their accustomed channels. Unknown to Casca in his deep sleep, other blood vessels had taken over the job of circulating his blood through his system, each minutely expanding and contracting and thus pumping the life-giving oxygen and nutrients to the places where they were needed most. In effect, his entire circulatory system was one diffuse temporary heart, adequate to sustain life while, bit by bit, his body took the steps needed to repair itself.

Casca woke.

The first thing he saw was a mass of thick black hair covering his chest. There was confusion for just a moment, then the mass of hair moved. Metah. She was lying on his chest, her hair covering him, and she was sleeping. Gently he raised his scarred hand and stroked her hair as he would a sleeping child.

"Little girl," he whispered, his voice ragged and unfamiliar from lack of use, "I love you."

She snuggled closer. . . .

The next few days brought an amazing change in him. With every breath he now drew, with every beat of the now-functioning heart, he grew stronger.

Totzin the priest wondered about the progress of the stranger. Casca's miraculous survival he attributed to an alliance between this foreigner and the hated priest of the Serpent, Tezmec.

Once Casca recovered he found himself in control of the city and the people, and every day he increased that control. The miracle of his survival and the godlike speed of his recovery would have set the stage for him in any event, but the way he was now twisting Tezmec around his little finger speeded up matters greatly. Something had happened to Tezmec since those incredible moments at the altar. He had no will to resist Casca. His thoughts were confused, but he watched in silent bewilderment as Casca stopped all human sacrifice and did nothing to hinder him. He did come in private to Casca and protest that surely disaster would strike his people, the rains would stop, and pestilence would stalk the land as it had done in the days of Cuz-mecli's father. But when the Tectli Casca would hear nothing of his reasons but merely stated flatly that the sacrifices must stop, Tezmec bowed his old head in obedience.

Even the warriors of the Serpent followed Casca's lead. They firmly aligned themselves with the living god that walked among them. Casca had more than adequately shown his superiority to all the warriors in the matter of combat and had defeated any who dared to face him in tests of strength and ability.

He was firmly in control.

Except for Totzin.

Only Totzin did not follow the will of Casca in all

things. And there were rumors. It was said that young girls who had disappeared were being offered to Teypetel the Jaguar under the blade of Totzin's dagger. Rumors, though. No proof.

The law concerning sacrifice was clear. Only captives in war or those who came voluntarily from among their own people could be used as messengers. To take maidens against their will was unthinkable, and, though Totzin was hostile to Tezmec, surely he would not break the laws of their people. No, the disappearance of the young women must be accounted for as the acts of raiders from some of the savage tribes living about them, young braves sneaking in to steal brides. It had happened before. Perhaps even the Toltecs could be responsible.

Meanwhile, Totzin carefully avoided any confrontation with Casca. When they did chance to meet, Totzin showed deference and servility. But deep behind his honeyed words his heart was black with hate—hate for this pale-skinned one who had by some conspiracy taken over control of Totzin's nation and proclaimed himself a god. Totzin had seen the runners sent by Casca to the coast where the rest of the accursed foreigner's men waited. Twice before Casca had sent runners, but Totzin's Jaguar soldiers had stopped them and offered their hearts to Teypetel. But the last runners had succeeded. Now more like Casca would come. And with them Totzin's power would decrease even more. The time was now. He must meet with the king of the Olmecs. Between them they could crush this evil that had come and deprived them of their just dues and respects. Soon the great jaws of the things. And there were rumors. It was said that young girls who had disappeared were being offered to Teypetel the Jaguar under the blade of Totzin's dagger. Rumors, though. No proof.

The law concerning sacrifice was clear. Only captives in war or those who came voluntarily from among their own people could be used as messengers. To take maidens against their will was unthinkable, and, though Totzin was hostile to Tezmec, surely he would not break the laws of their people. No, the disappearance of the young women must be accounted for as the acts of raiders from some of the savage tribes living about them, young braves sneaking in to steal brides. It had happened before. Perhaps even the Toltecs could be responsible.

Meanwhile, Totzin carefully avoided any confrontation with Casca. When they did chance to meet, Totzin showed deference and servility. But deep behind his honeyed words his heart was black with hate—hate for this pale-skinned one who had by some conspiracy taken over control of Totzin's nation and proclaimed himself a god. Totzin had seen the runners sent by Casca to the coast where the rest of the accursed foreigner's men waited. Twice before Casca had sent runners, but Totzin's Jaguar soldiers had stopped them and offered their hearts to Teypetel. But the last runners had succeeded. Now more like Casca would come. And with them Totzin's power would decrease even more. The time was now. He must meet with the king of the Olmecs. Between them they could crush this evil that had come and deprived them of their just dues and respects. Soon the great jaws of the

Totzin the priest wondered about the progress of the stranger. Casca's miraculous survival he attributed to an alliance between this foreigner and the hated priest of the Serpent, Tezmec.

Once Casca recovered he found himself in control of the city and the people, and every day he increased that control. The miracle of his survival and the godlike speed of his recovery would have set the stage for him in any event, but the way he was now twisting Tezmec around his little finger speeded up matters greatly. Something had happened to Tezmec since those incredible moments at the altar. He had no will to resist Casca. His thoughts were confused, but he watched in silent bewilderment as Casca stopped all human sacrifice and did nothing to hinder him. He did come in private to Casca and protest that surely disaster would strike his people, the rains would stop, and pestilence would stalk the land as it had done in the days of Cuz-mecli's father. But when the Tectli Casca would hear nothing of his reasons but merely stated flatly that the sacrifices must stop, Tezmec bowed his old head in obedience.

Even the warriors of the Serpent followed Casca's lead. They firmly aligned themselves with the living god that walked among them. Casca had more than adequately shown his superiority to all the warriors in the matter of combat and had defeated any who dared to face him in tests of strength and ability.

He was firmly in control.

Except for Totzin.

Only Totzin did not follow the will of Casca in all

had made a cart of clay with wheels that rolled. The children were delighted. Casca decided this would be a good way to teach the people the use of the wheel for heavy transport, for, although the idea of the wheel was known, it was not used here for the obvious purpose. Casca demonstrated the ability of the wheel to haul heavy loads. Demonstrated—but that was all. God or no god, he got nowhere with the people; they merely smiled, agreed—and went back to doing things as they always had, hauling their loads on their backs with a strap about the forehead to keep it in position.

While Casca busied himself with the load-carrying activities of the people of Teotah, however, in the land of the Olmecs quite a different kind of traffic was going on. The loads being brought into the Olmec cities were not food nor articles of trade. They were tribute from the villages in the Olmec domain, tribute in the form of weapons: spears and axes and clubs sided with flint; deer horn shields; and quilted suits of cotton armor. The king of the Olmecs had arrived at a decision: he would march on the city of Teotah. His ego had been bruised by the reports he had received of the Quetza's great strength. That and the opportunity to have warriors loyal to his cause already within the city was too much to pass up. He would prove to all that he was the greatest warrior in the world. After Teotah he would march against all who opposed his divinity. He would leave his monuments behind: the great heads of his and his father's likenesses, fat lips sneering in a grin that showed teeth filed to needle points (as the teeth of the jaguar were pointed, so jungle hunter, the killer of men, would have all the blood he needed. The god Teypetel would feed to the fullest, and he, Totzin, would himself offer the body of Casca to the god—and if the stranger's heart still beat after the blade, then he would slice him into a thousand separate pieces and feed them one by one to the vultures. That would take care of even the Quetza.

Totzin sent runners secretly to the stronghold of the giant king of the Olmecs. Following Totzin's instructions, they offered their master's allegiance if the great Olmec king would come to their aid and rid their city of the foreigner, for surely, was not the great king of the Olmecs the only one powerful enough to stand against the blue-eyed one in combat? And if he did this, would not the wealth of the Teotec nation be his? And, with Totzin as his suzerain, there would be sent him an unending stream of victims for the glory of the Jaguar.

Casca had grown used to being a god and was beginning to enjoy it. On his tours around the city he gained an ever greater appreciation of what these people had accomplished. They had no weapons of metal to speak of. The only ones they did have were poor things beaten out of native raw copper ore. They apparently lacked the knowledge of how to refine the ore itself. But gold and silver were plentiful and they used these metals for the glory of their gods. The metal gold seemed to them to have no value other than its easy pliability in the manufacture of sacred artifacts and art objects.

Casca discovered what many another innovator had before him and since—that it is not easy to change a people's technology. For the children he must his be). The decision made, the king rose from his throne and gave orders to his captains to make ready. When the moon was full they would march.

And on the coast, other men were already marching.

The runners had finally gotten through to the dragon ships. The Vikings had the word from Casca and had set out to rejoin their leader. They were not aware of what a strange sight they made in this land . . . large men with tanned skins and hair of many colors, their armor gleaming in the sun, helmets with the horns of beasts on them . . . strong men who cursed at every step that took them away from the security of the sea and their only link with their homes, the dragon ships that had brought them safely thus far. But their master called, and they obeyed, leaving the dragon ships in the care of warriors bearing the emblem of a snake and of such few Vikings who were too ill or too injured to make the journey to the city where Casca the Walker was a god.

Olaf Glamson, however, relished the change—and the chance for action. His high spirits and laughter did much to dispel the gloom that many of his countrymen felt in these forbidding jungles.

Every step took them closer. Word of their coming reached Casca while he was with the young king. Casca and the king were fast becoming great friends. Casca liked the young man for his spirit and courage. The youngster was eager to meet these approaching strangers, for the Quetza had said that with them came a new order. And Cuz-mecli, though he had believed in the need for it since that was his teaching, had never really liked the sight of men's hearts being torn from them. Now, if the gods were all like the Quetza, surely it would be better for his people. He had seen no disaster befall them since the sacrifices had stopped. The rains still came, and the people prospered and were content. They gloried that only they, of all peoples, had a god living with them.

As for Metah, she gloried in her man. Casca took no other women and seemed to be content with her. She was always at his side. The close association brought a subtle change: she grew more beautiful every day, carrying herself as if she had to the royal manor been born. She was the consort of a god . . . but she knew him as a man. . . .

The days were warm and good. Casca walked among his people, watching the women spin, watching them turn the spindles to convert the cotton wool into thread for cloth. The young children were learning the arts of their fathers . . . to be either warriors or priests. But the ones who really made the city live were the farmers, merchants, and artisans. Casca took a special delight in the workers of stone and gold. Watching a goldsmith refining his precious metal, Casca noted that there was no difference in the method here from that of his own homeland, Rome. The gold was stacked in earthenware plates and placed in a pot, each plate separated by powdered stone or brick dust. Then the pot was covered and heated until it glowed red. The smith would build up the heat with a blowing bellows until the gold was hot enough to melt. The impurities would combine with the dust, and when the process was finished the gold was purified and ready to be worked.

Casca was thus absorbed in watching the goldsmith when the runner came and fell to his knees before the Quetza.

"Lord," the runner reported, "they come! The giant and the ones with the shining skins come as you ordered."

The Vikings had reached Teotah.

ELEVEN

The sight that greeted the Vikings was one that they knew they would long remember. Those who lived would tell and retell to their children and grandchildren what they saw that day. To begin with, they were properly awed by the size of the great city, and by the buildings. But that was only the beginning. When they reached the great square and were surrounded by palaces and pyramids, the sight left them all with their mouths hanging open —unfortunately an invitation to the Teotec flies. Ten thousand warriors lined the square, each in the brilliant plumage of his sect. Foremost, by virtue of their allegiance to Casca, were the Serpent men. Then the Jaguar soldiers. Less prominent were the Coyote troops and the Puma sect, but even these were grouped together in a brilliant rainbow display of feathers and skins. Their faces were painted, their weapons edged with obsidian and flint, their shields bearing designs strange and wonderful to the Vikings and tassled with exotic feathers.

Nor was the sight alone all. Then came the sound of drums and reed flutes. The group of Serpent soldiers to the west drew back to form a lane—and the Vikings gawked in amazement. Here came a giant litter carried by fifty men, their faces black and each naked as the day he was born. They moved and chanted in step, carrying their enormous burden. The litter was protected by a canopy. Seated on a throne under the canopy was a monstrous figure in gleaming feathers, his face covered by a green stone mask, his hands holding a spear and one of the wooden clubs edged with razor-sharp obsidian.

People by the tens of thousands stood lining the thoroughfares as far as the eye could see. They were all quiet and well-behaved. When the palanquin approached, they would prostrate themselves to it.

The litter was definitely the center of attention. As it drew closer, the Vikings could see that it was covered with sheets of gold and decorated with blue and green stones. An ancient priest preceded it. His staff of office aided him to walk. His head was erect and proud beneath his coating of red and black paint. Closer the giant litter came. The drumming and the fluting reaching an ear-piercing crescendo as they neared. Ten feet from the Vikings they stopped. The sudden silence was impressive. It was broken for the Vikings only by the sound of their own breathing. Then a voice boomed out at them.

"Welcome!" it said in the language of the Norsemen. "Welcome to the lands and city of the

Teotec."

Olaf stared in amazament. "Is it you, lord, behind the green mask? Aye. It must be. None of these people has eyes of your color. By Odin, lord, you look like some great green bird in all those feathers. Surely you sit in a strange nest. But we are glad to see you, lord, and, as you have ordered, we have come to do your bidding."

In the Roman manner taught them by Casca, the Vikings drew their swords at Olaf's command and with the wind whipping through the blond and red mustaches cried out as one man: "Hail, Casca, Lord of the Keep! Ave! Ave!"

Casca signaled, and the junior priests lowered their burden carefully to the ground. He stepped to the front of the litter.

His barbaric splendor was a sight to see. On his arms and wrists he wore bracelets of gold in the likeness of serpents eating their tails, while around his neck a massive pendant of beaten gold inlaid with jade pictured the history of the Teotec.

He removed the mask. It was beginning to cramp him anyway. His familiar scarred face, red and sweating, smiled at his men.

Sweeping Olaf up in his arms, Casca roared with obvious pleasure. He thumped Olaf on his back until the young Glamson thought his ribs would give way.

"Pray, lord," he pleaded, "if you would have me in any condition to fight later on, go easy now."

Casca's rolling laughter echoed around the square, and the sound of his mirth set the native people to smiling. All was well. The Tectli was pleased. Passing through the ranks of his men,

Casca called each by name. He asked about the faces that were missing and frowned at their loss. But the life of a soldier is death, and they had died like men. When the living returned to their home fires even the dead would become immortal in the telling and retelling of great feats.

Returning to his litter, Casca called out to the city: "These are my men! They are to be your friends! They shall live among you! But, remember, they are not of your ways and customs. Be patient with them, and they will learn. If any offends, you tell me, and I will administer justice. These are my words. So let it be. I am the Quetza."

Turning to Olaf, he said, "You will be made welcome. Quarters are prepared. You and your men must rest after your journey. Come to me for the evening meal. Bring your officers, and we will talk of what must be done here."

Olaf was properly astounded. He bowed his head. "As you wish, my lord." Then he turned to his hairy band, and his voice boomed out in command—very much like Casca:

"Let none here offend our hosts by bad manners. Though these people appear to be savage, I think we could learn much from them. The first one of you who gets his ass in trouble—particularly over a woman—will find himself singing his death song a helluva lot quicker than he thought. Understand? Good! Then follow these men." He indicated the priests who had stepped forward at Casca's bidding. "We will rest."

Once at their assigned quarters, the Vikings settled down to an excited chatter about their new surroundings and about what had happened to

Casca. While this was going on a group of women slaves, heads bowed, demure, entered. Each went to one of the warriors and put a necklace of gold and turquoise about his neck, then a bracelet of gold set with jade on his wrist. Shy and fearful, they then withdrew. After getting a good look at the asses of the slave girls, several of the Vikings were immediately ready to trade their gifts for a quickie.

"All right, settle down." Olaf's voice came through the excitement. "You men hit the sack. But before you go to sleep, make sure your weapons are clean and ready for use. Also, I want three men posted at the entrance at all times. We may be guests here, but we should be careful as always."

Totzin had watched the proceedings with the bile bitter in his mouth. *Well enough*, he thought. *More of these paleskins for the altars.* His eyes caught a glimpse of Metah as she joined Casca on his litter for the return to the palace. Totzin ran his tongue over his lips as he watched the rich sway of her hips and the bounce of her ripe breasts. *When I am done with the Quetza, I shall take her for my own as long as she pleases me. When she no longer amuses me, I shall feed her to the Jaguar . . . except for those parts I take for myself. . . .*

Olaf followed his painted priest guide across the way to the palace of Casca. His quick gaze missed nothing. He was taken past guards in elaborate headdresses and with strange weapons. The walls were covered with murals depicting the life and culture of the people of Teotah. Behind Olaf his officers followed him in awe. Finally they came to a massive door of carved wood. Two Serpent soldiers opened it and ushered the Vikings into a more familiar presence.

Casca stood in the center of the huge room wearing only a loincloth. His arms and wrists were covered by massive gold bracelets. Casca welcomed the Vikings. They stood for a moment looking around the room. In the center were benches and a table covered with many foods—even the flesh of the small dog that these people prized so much.

"Before we talk, eat and drink," Casca commanded. He indicated for them to take their places with a sweep of his muscled arms. The movement of his arms focused attention on the jagged scar on his chest, the raised red welt that had not yet had time to pale into the many other faded scars that limned his body. Olaf eyed the jagged wound but said nothing. Casca would tell of it when he was ready—but now for the food. The Norsemen fell to with their normal vigor, though most of them carefully avoided the red peppers and spices. They had met those on their journey, and just looking at them they could remember how they had burned their mouths . . . and even later the burning was renewed when the chiles made their exit. The meat they favored most was that of a large bird resembling a giant chicken, but with drumsticks twice the size of that familiar domestic fowl.

The men showed a definite liking for the local wine, once they got used to the taste. Casca told them it was called octli. There was also the more pungent mezcal. A few of the Vikings even swore to its good effects. Both, Casca explained, came from a fleshy, long-leaved plant with sharp spines that was known as the magucy.

Olaf swallowed a long draw of pulque, wiped his blond mustache clean with the back of his hand, and said, "Well, Lord Casca, it may not be beer or mead, but it does set your head feeling as if all were well. Is it?"

The question cut through the clamor.

"Well enough, Olaf Glamson."

They all stopped eating. Casca looked around at the waiting, expectant faces of those who had followed him so far from their home waters. One by one he gazed into their eyes, into the faces of these, his officers. They were rough men with the blood of heroes in their veins, not the refined cultured officers of the Roman nobility nor of the princes of the East. These men could spend a lifetime without sleeping under a roof and feel no sense of deprivation. They could eat anything that walked, flew, dug, or swam—or that could eat them, and they'd even take that on if they got in the first bite. Their form of courage was basic and primitive in its origin. They had been raised on a steady diet of what they believed to be the manly virtues. Courage and loyalty to their own came first. Their own lives were less important to them than being faithful to what they considered to be their honor as warriors.

Beside Olaf sat Vlad the Dark. His hair was coal black, with traces of blue lights in it. His skin was deep bronze from the sun. He could almost have been taken for one of the Teotecs had it not been for the piercing blue eyes that watched all about him in quiet study. Quiet he was, and the most mannerly of the barbarians seated here. Seldom did he get into the piss-binding drunken stupor that his comrades seemed to enjoy so much. Nor was the Viking habit of boasting his. He never sang his own praises nor boasted of his prowess with the great axe. Yet few intentionally offended him. The foolish ones who did soon found themselves without their uppermost appendage, for Vlad's quiet manners belied his swiftness with axe and sword. Only to Olaf—whom he loved like an elder brother—and to Casca, the Lord of the Keep, did he show deference.

The other Vikings were cut more from the cloth of rude violence and boisterous spirits. Bjornson, Olvir, and Swey were very much like Holdbod the Berserker. When Holdbod fought, the rage would come over him. His lips would froth. He would scream in what seemed an unknown tongue, literally crying for more to come, and slaughtering those who did with his great two-handed blade that was larger than one most half-grown youths could even raise to the waist. With this great sword he could split a man from crown to the waist as clean as a butcher would carve beef.

Casca completed his mental survey. These, then, were his men. He addressed them.

"Olaf, we will soon have work to do. Messengers have come to me that the king of the lands adjoining Teotah is preparing to march against us. And, while I have the loyalty of most of this city, there are some whose mouths speak well, but whose eyes and actions lie."

Olaf broke in, "But, lord, why should we involve ourselves with these people's fights? Why don't we just take what we will and set sail for home? Surely from what I have seen here there is gold and silver enough to make us all rich as kings. What are these people to us?"

Casca caught hold of his temper. His voice dropped a register.

"Olaf, I love you for yourself and for your father. But this is my will. These people and this city are now mine and they are my responsibility. They have the makings of a greater nation than any I have ever met, but they must have time to grow. Here I have stopped the sacrificing of human beings to their gods, and they look on me as a god. I have taken away from them something they held sacred for centuries. And more . . . I have found a woman. There are other reasons, but these will suffice."

Casca's gray gaze forced Olaf's eyes down.

"Aye, lord. We have sworn to obey you in all things. If this is your wish, then so it be. We are your men," Glamson replied.

Pleased, Casca responded in gentler tones: "Olaf, after the fighting is done, those who wish may take the longships and sail for home. And, as you say, each man will have enough gold to make him rich as a king. But before that time, each must earn his reward. When the Olmecs are beaten, I will release you from your oath of fealty."

"Very good, my lord. But, if there will be slaughter, then perhaps you will have need of this."

Reaching under the table, Olaf pulled the sack he had been carrying when they entered into full view. It was bulky. It clanged as he set it on the table, sweeping aside trays and plates with his arm, clearing a spot.

Olaf reached inside the bag and pulled out, one

at a time, items that each evoked a memory of Casca's past. First, there was a full set of Roman armor. It was the set Casca had in his pack when he and Olaf's father, old Glam, had fought for and won the keep in which Olaf was born. It was well-used armor, but it had been even better cared for.

Olaf held up each piece of the armor for his leader's appraisal. The only new piece was the tunic of white linen with half sleeves and a skirt reaching to the knees. The cuirass was of three parts. The shoulder epaulets and the chest and back covering were all made of boiled, formed leather on which were sewn circular pieces of iron. The shoulder pieces were made of four plates, smaller than those of the cuirass to which they were fixed on the ends and passed over the shoulders like straps. From the waist were two thick borders of leather plated with strips of iron reaching almost to the knees.

As each piece was brought out and presented, Casca felt a rush of memories.

"One last item, lord," Olaf said. "This was dropped when the cat soldiers took you captive. For some reason they left it where it lay."

Reaching deep into the sack, Olaf withdrew Casca's famous short sword. The weapon had been meticulously cleaned and sharpened. Not a spot of rust would dare make itself known on the shining surface. The blade had been honed on both sides to razor sharpness. There were, however, several deep notches in the blade that gave it a slightly serrated appearance. They had been too deep to remove without damaging the rest of the sword.

Casca took the weapon in his calloused hand.

The grip felt alive. He had carried this weapon ever since he had left the battlefield in Parthia where the city of Ctesiphon had been put to the sword. How many years had it been? Fifty? Sixty? More?

Casca put his free hand on the forearm of Olaf. "Thank you. This weapon is more than a tool. It is the story of my life. It and my destiny are one. Thank you, Olaf Glamson. Now I must go. Even a god has duties, and several await me. You and the others, eat and enjoy yourselves. Tomorrow we begin to ready for the battle."

That night, while the Norsemen slept, they were closer to war than they imagined. Even now, while they were tossing in their sleep and dreaming of the women they had left at home, Teypetel was being borne on a giant litter carried by eighty slaves at the front of his army. Thirty thousand strong the enemy marched. The litter bearers were changed and replaced by fresh slaves every three miles. Less if the going was rough.

In Teotah, the city of the Teotec, only Totzin knew what was transpiring, and he slept the best sleep of all. Victory was soon to be in his grasp, and the city and its people would be his. The few foreign devils who had come could make no possible difference in the outcome. Five days, and the king of the Olmecs and his army would be at the doors of Teotah. Then the god of the Jaguar would feed to the fullest. He, Totzin, would see to it that the one calling himself the Quetza performed no further tricks or illusions. He smiled as he slept. A warm, wet flash ran down his leg from the groin as he dreamed of what he would do to the woman of the Quetza. Not all his excitement was sexual in nature; the thought of feeding himself on her flesh was as strong a stimulant as the sex act itself.

Dawn brought no indications of the coming violence.

Casca sat and breakfasted with the king and Tezmec.

"Priest," he asked, "why do your cities have no walls for defense?"

Tezmec smiled and spoke in the same tone of voice he used in teaching novices. "The jungles and hills are our walls. We have scouts out on every trail leading to our city. If an enemy approaches, it is from the walls of the jungle that we meet and strike them before they can reach us. In the event that the enemy manages to break through to the city itself, then our people use those same jungle walls to hide in, taking with them their items of most value.

"The enemy takes an empty city. From the hills and jungles we will strike down and attack his warriors. When they learn the cost is too great they will return to their own lands, and we will come back. At the most, they will have taken the items left behind, but these are of no real value. What use can they make of cooking pots? The value is in the people. Without them there can be no real victory. If they destroy our temples, then we will simply build greater and larger ones when they are gone, and when the time is right. We will avenge ourselves. Our people would never accept a foreign king. He must be one of our own."

The young king nodded in agreement. "Is it not so in the lands you said are across the waters, Tectli Quetza?"

Casca shook his shaggy head in denial. "No," he said, "it is not. Perhaps your way is better for you, but the people I know are different. There we need the walls to defend ourselves. Perhaps even here you will one day find a need for them."

The Olmecs and their grotesque king were now only four days away from Teotah. On this day the passes leading to the city were guarded by Serpent soldiers. Tomorrow the guard would change; the soldiers of the Jaguar would take over the duty of watching the far passes through which the enemy must pass.

Casca paid ever increasing attention to his troops the next days. More and more he drilled them in new methods of fighting, methods new to them but old to the legions of Caesar. His Vikings would be the anvil against which any invader would smash themselves; his regular Teotec soldiers would be the hammer.

Totzin smiled, especially when he saw Casca with Metah. *Enjoy the woman while you can,* he thought. *Soon it will be the trust of my loins that she screams out for.*

Teypetel entered the valley, his army strung out behind, not yet in battle order. Cautiously his scouts proceeded and returned, prostrating themselves before their king and giving the word that the way was clear; the Jaguar soldiers of the priest Totzin had honored their word and were even now coming down to join the army. Their remaining brothers in the city would strike from the inside when the time was ripe. The way was open, and soldiers of the Olmecs poured through, faces painted for war. Many had the same flat lips and noses of their king, for he and his fathers had spread their seed wherever they could. The cast of brutality was clearly stamped on them.

Casca sat late in his rooms. Metah walked softly so as not to disturb him. She knew that he had many things on his mind. He sat alone looking out over his city. The flat roofs and the temple pyramids seemed frozen in the light of the brilliant moon and the cloudless sky. His thoughts reached across the dark waters, far, far to another land, Rome. Rome . . . *It has been long since I saw the city of Caesar Augustus.* He still referred to it as the city of the man who sat on the throne of the world's most powerful nation when he, Casca, was young and first served in the legion. Who was emperor now? How much longer would Rome endure? Or had she already fallen to internal rot and the bright swords of the more vital peoples surrounding her?

Rome. . . . Now he understood a little of what the Caesars must have endured. The weight of responsibility is heavy for a ruler. *I wonder why they, the power seekers, crave it so much?*

There were, of course, things that Casca could not know. While he ruled the Teotec not as king but as god, Rome was moving ever closer to her final days. It had been 253 years since the so-called "Messiah" had died on the Cross. Valerian was once again trying to stabilize the frontiers of the Empire. He had made his son Gallienus emperor of the west while he marched to the east to try and restore order. He was too late. Ever increasingly, better organized and more violent rebellions had sapped the spirits of the legions along the Danube. They were now facing the new confederation of the Gothic Empire. The borders were crumbling. The Goths laid to the sword much of Asia Minor and even northern Greece. Valerian was taken prisoner by the persians.

This same night Valerian's son Gallienus sat with the thoughts of disaster foremost in his mind. He had retaken the Balkans, but his strength was so limited that Gaul, Spain, the Rhineland—and even Britain—paid homage only to their autonomous rulers. Gallienus sighed deeply. The weight of Rome was heavy. He pondered the responsibilities of power as he poured another draught of the famous Falerian wine, sipped slowly, and cut it with a touch of spring water. Finishing his cup, he called for his masseur to come and rub away some of the tensions of the day. *Rome may be fading, but that is no excuse to live like a barbarian. . . .*

TWELVE

Casca clicked his eyes back open. He shook his head. He had been asleep and dreaming. . . . Or had he? What was the matter?

Shit! I know something is wrong. Totzin is walking around like he is the cat that just swallowed the mouse. Something is rotten. Tomorrow I'll send out my own scouts to take a look around the countryside.

Casca slept, the warm body and soft hair of Metah his only coverlet in the warm night. Mumbling in her sleep, she snuggled closer.

The first light of dawn saw Casca up and about, waking his men and sending the runners out to the far passes. Tezmec, too, was up early. On a temple, unseen, he was praying for forgiveness and divine guidance, bowing low before the sun rising from the basin surrounding them. He was singing the ancient songs of his race. The carved figures of the Serpent and Tlaloc seemed to mock him. He received no answer. Weary from his long vigil, he took his old bones back down from the pyramid to his home. The day was almost upon them.

Casca's Vikings were rousing themselves from various stages of sleep and stupefaction. Those who had chosen women were running them off so they could be about their master's work for the day. Platters of venison, half-cooked, charred on the outside, were being gulped down, along with the flat cakes called tortillas.

Casca stood with the young king instructing him in the use of the short sword, explaining that weapons didn't just happen; they were designed to serve the style or battle and other accouterments of the user. Patiently answering Cuz-mecli's questions, he explained that the short sword was designed to stab around and beneath even when the opponent had a longer weapon and greater strength. If he could be forced to close with you, the shorter blade would give good service while the longer blade of the enemy was almost useless.

This discourse was broken up when the bloody figure of a Serpent soldier stumbled into their presence and threw himself down before Casca and the king, a feathered barb protruding from his back. Bloody froth on his lips showed that he was shot in the lung.

His painted face was raised painfully.

"Tectli Casca . . . . They came . . . the Olmecs. They are through the pass and even now are less than an hour from the city. Their king, Teypetel, the monster, leads them. . . ."

The man shivered as if from a sudden chill, gave one short cough, and was still. He was the first victim of the war between the Teotec and the Olmec.

First blood was the Olmec's, but, swore Casca, not the last.

Tezmec stepped in front of the king and Casca. He had been coming in the entrance to the king's chambers when the runner appeared.

He pointed a withered finger at Casca. "I knew disaster would befall us," he accused. "You have betrayed us! Because of you, many of my people will perish. It is too late to hide in the hills. We must have sacrifices to appease the gods and prevent this disaster from befalling us!"

Casca faced the old priest.

"No! By all the hounds of hell, no! There will be no more hearts cut out on your bloody altar for your bloody gods!" Pushing roughly past the startled old priest, Casca strode to the balcony and bellowed like the mythical bull of the German forest, "Olaf!"

"Olaf!" he thundered, the name echoing around the great plaza. "Bring me my men!" Men . . . men . . . men. . . . The words repeated and faded.

The army of the Teotecs was gathered. Not all could make it in time, but fifteen thousand men stood ready, brilliant in their war dress and painted faces. They stood in silent ranks waiting for the one who would lead them in battle. In the city were Olaf and the Vikings, and the indication that today was different from others was mirrored in Vlad's face, which seemed a little darker. Holdbod fingered the edge of his great sword a little more frequently. They all waited like faithful hounds for their master's appearance.

Then he was before them.

The great Serpent helmet of feathers and gold

seemed to set off the armor of Rome that he wore.

Casca, Lord of the Keep, the Quetza of the Teotec stood before them.

The silence was oppressive.

And then, all at once, fifteen thousand voices cried out:

"Quetza!

"Quetza!

"Quetza!"

The roaring thunder of the name increased with each breath until it seemed the very force of their calling would bring down the walls of the buildings even before the Olmec had a chance at them. The Vikings, too, were taken up in this outpouring of fervor. Banging their steel swords against their shields, they tried to drown out the cries of the Teotec warriors with their even louder "Ave, Casca! Lord of the Keep! Ave, Casca, Lord of the Keep!"

Casca raised his recently reacquired short sword above his head and motioned for silence. He was obeyed. In the language of the Teotec he gave the command for the captains to come forth for orders. Gathering his leaders to him, he first ordered the captain of the Jaguars to take up positions behind the pyramid of the sun. From there they would strike on the signal given by a giant conch shell. Dismissing the Jaguar soldier, and waiting until he was out of earshot, Casca then turned to Olaf and his men.

"Vikings," he ordered, "you will place yourselves in the rear of the Serpent soldiers and hold your position."

Olaf started to grumble, but was quickly cut

short by Casca's terse "Obey!"

"Yes, my lord." Olaf fumed at the idea that the Vikings might be left out of the main thrust of the coming battle, but he followed his orders.

Casca then ordered a squad of Serpent men to take the king to the hills outside and not to return until he sent known runners to bring the word that all was well. Those who could would follow from among the women and children, but all men must stand ready to fight whether they were capable of standing on their own two feet or not. These would mount the rooftops with stones and anything else they could throw down on the heads of the invaders.

The Coyote soldiers were to be on the right flank with the remaining miscellaneous troups covering the rest of the right. The Serpents were to hold the center; theirs was the place of honor. Casca dismissed his captains. He wished that he had Avidius Cassius here to borrow his brain for a moment. Avidius might have been a butcher, but the son-of-a-bitch knew how to plan and organize a battle. *Shit, I'm okay for small unit actions, but I never had to deal with anything like this.* . . . Self-doubt afflicted Casca. *Well, all I can do is the best I can, but it won't be anything fancy.*

The Olmecs were coming into sight. From the tops of the highest buildings the faint-hearted already had begun their death wails—which Casca soon stopped with the order to cut the throat of anyone who made a sound he didn't authorize. Separating a few of the toughest-looking troops, he positioned them on the exits and avenues leading off the plaza. He wanted the Olmecs to stay where he could keep an eye on them. *Where the Hades are Tezmec and Totzin?* Part of his question was answered as he saw the high priest of the Jaguar standing in full regalia watching the proceedings from his temple top. *Well enough. That's a good place for the shriveled-up little bastard.* But of Tezmec there was no sign.

Giving orders right and left, Casca raced around the square checking on his men and their leaders. Making sure his Vikings were in position, he gave his final orders . . . leaving Olaf with a smile on his face.

Teypetel sat on his litter, an obscenely fat, royal gargoyle. He wore only a robe made from the hide of the great spotted cat he held holy. Otherwise he was naked. The eighty slaves carrying his monster litter strained and sweated under the lash of his priest soldiers. They crested a small rise, and there before them lay the city of Teotah.

Teypetel's fat lips pulled back from his gums, exposing the needle teeth. He ran his tongue over the sharp teeth as if already tasting the blood that would flow so freely from the bodies to be slaughtered by his soldiers and him this day.

Teypetel gave his orders to his commanders. The Olmecs spread out on the plains facing the city, forming an arc tapering to the ends but thickened in the center. The Olmec plan was to use the points of the arc to encircle and outflank Casca's forces while the strong center smashed into the Teotec and kept them concentrated there until the horns of the arc reached each other and the encirclement was complete. Teypetel knew he had numerical superiority on his side; that and the aid of the Jaguar soldiers loyal to the would-be priest-king Totzin were enough to guarantee victory.

Now, surely the Teotec must be aware of his presence. They would be in a panic to get their troops organized and ready for fighting. That combined with what must surely be the panic of the civilian population would greatly hinder the efforts of the city to defend itself.

Smiling at the thought of the panic that his approach must be bringing, Teypetel ordered his drums to begin—drums so large it took six slaves to carry each. The drums were positioned every two hundred feet in the rear of his troops. On his signal, they beat as one, a terrible rolling sound, like thunder in the valley.

The sound of distant thunder reaching the defenders in the city confused them. The skies were clear. Was this an ill omen?

Casca looked to the sound, the sun sparkling off his brilliant feathered robe, the same robe he had worn on the day of his sacrifice. Shading his eyes with his right hand he watched the soldiers of the Olmecs spread out and begin to move in toward the city. From this distance the invading army looked like the horns of one of the African bulls he had seen in the arena at Rome. To the rear of the soldiers he could just make out the huge drums and their attendants. *So that's what's going on.* Relaying to his men below that the thunder was only caused by giant drums, he ran down to the square. Taking a thousand warriors with him, he raced to the city's edge where the broad avenue stopped and the lesser trails began.

The enemy was approaching through the tall fields and the rows of cultivated, spiked maguey plants. Lining his warriors in three ranks, Casca waited. The drumming sound was almost overpowering. Steadily the Olmec approached. One hundred of the thousand warriors Casca had taken were archers. By his standards they were nothing to compare with the archers of the Scythians and Parthians. They lacked the laminated bows of those famous fighters. The Teotec bows were lighter, and they were shooting arrows of cane from the marshes, tipped with sharpened bits of stone. But they were what he had, and he planned to use them. He had the archers stationed behind the rearmost rank of warriors.

Carefully, Casca watched his men for any sign of panic. They were standing fast, the ruddy, square faces composed and placid. Never had a Roman commanded an army of such brilliance. With their feathered headdresses and plumed wicker shields, the warriors seemed more like terrible beasts or birds than mere men. They carried deadly weapons. Their lances were tipped with flint and obsidian. Their clubs were edged with the same razor-sharp stones. The nobles among them each vyed with the others in their elaborate war suits. Many wore enough gold and precious stones to set even an avaricious Caesar's mouth watering with envy. They waited, confident. After all, they had a god with them.

The Olmec stopped their approach one hundred yards from the soldiers of the Teotec. Their drums were silent. The sudden stillness had a strange, eerie quality.

Casca advanced out from his line of warriors to where he was clearly visible, escorted by only one Serpent soldier, the escort carrying one of the spears he had been given by Vlad the Dark when Vlad learned he was to be one of Casca's bodyguards. Vlad had insisted on the man taking the Viking spear.

Casca walked slowly. The Roman cuirass seemed to be a second skin, except there was still one place over the ribs on his left side where a knot of thread holding the metal discs affixed cut into his skin, slowly wearing a sore spot. *Shit,* he thought, *I meant to have that fixed. The damn thing's going to hurt all day.*

Filling his lungs with air and raising his right arm in salute, Casca bellowed out:

"Teypetel! Dog king of the Olmec! Come forth!"

Casca's voice clearly reached Teypetel.

Stunned, with surprising agility Teypetel leaped from his litter. *Dog! He dares call me a dog!* Never in all his life had anyone dared to insult Teypetel. Not even his mother. For she knew full well that he would have cut her heart out and eaten it as he had done to his own brothers when they contested his right to the throne.

Pushing his way through to the front ranks, Teypetel stood there, gross, huge, his breasts like those of a fat woman. He towered over every one of his warriors by at least a head. His arms were larger than the thighs of his biggest and strongest warrior. His skin was oiled. In his right hand he carried a battleaxe of native copper, hand-beaten, and as large as the skull of a deer. Using the instrument to bash the brains out of a soldier who was too slow in moving out of his way, he reached the foremost rank and stepped out.

Casca took a look at his opponent. *Shit,* he thought, *that is one large hunk of suet.*

A distance of two hundred feet separated them.

Teypetel, too, sized up the man confronting him. From this distance Casca did not seem so godlike . . . even if he did wear strange armor. . . .

Teypetel's white pointed teeth sparkled. "Are you the one called the Quetza?" His speech had a slight sibilance to it caused by the sharpened teeth.

Casca stepped out a few more steps.

"Yes, molester of small boys and dogs, I am the Quetza."

Taken aback by the repeated offense and wondering, *How did he know about the dogs?* Teypetel paused. But quick anger rose to his face, making his head feel as though he had drunk too much pulque, and in that anger he caved in the skull of his own nearest guard. The brains splattered on his feet. He roared: "Come forth and fight! Let us do battle here." Even in his rage he was rational enough to note that in the open his troops could easily butcher the few warriors with the one called Quetza.

Casca laughed, his voice sneering as he replied: "No such deal, lard ass. You come to us. *If* you have the guts. And from here I can see that you have enough for at least six fat women."

Enraged, Teypetel broke the neck of a novice priest who had come too close to his massive right hand. Summoning his captains to him, Teypetel began to give them explicit orders that the foreigner was to be taken alive.

While this was going on, Casca took the spear from his aide. It was a good weapon, iron-tipped, stout ash stock. Expelling a deep breath in a long controlled burst as the shaft left his hand, Casca hurled the spear. It arced across the distance between him and the Olmec king.

Teypetel looked up in time to see the shaft arcing toward him, giving him a hell of a fright. He threw the leader of his center forces in front of him. The iron blade went into the warrior's back and protruded a full arm's length from his chest, the point of the spear stopping just short of the Olmec king who quickly scuttled back to the rear ranks. No one could throw a spear that far. Not one that heavy. . . .

Aw, crap. Missed him, Casca thought.

As Teypetel retreated, Casca's jeering voice followed, taunting: "What's the matter, lard ass? Afraid?"

Reaching the safety of his rear ranks, Teypetel screamed in blind fury: "Kill them! Attack!"

The legions of the Olmec obeyed. They raced to overrun the few pitiful soldiers who confronted them, their voices rising in animal cries. Predominant was the call of the hunting jaguar. The drums urged them on.

The center of the Olmecs moved in to crush Casca's force, and the horns began their pincer movement. But Teypetel had miscalculated. The wings were in confusion. They could move—but to where? They could not surround the whole city. The buildings would break up their formation. So they waited.

The center closed to one hundred feet, and when they did, Casca gave the order for his men to fall flat on their faces while the archers behind loosed waves of arrows over them straight into the faces and bodies of the overconfident Olmecs. The thin reed arrows found their way into the eyes and open mouths of many screaming warriors. The Olmecs paused. Casca leaped to his feet and ordered his men to conduct a fighting withdrawal. They led the Olmecs deeper and deeper into the confines of the city along the broad, building-banked thoroughfare. Casca and his men would run back to get ahead of the Olmecs for a space, then fall to the prone position as the archers let fly another wave of arrows. Leapfrogging in this manner they hurt the Olmecs, not enough to stop them, but enough to drive them wild with frustration.

Gradually Casca led back to where the main body of his army waited. The Olmecs would have run two or more miles, while his own troops would be fresh for the fight. It could make a difference, equalizing Casca's disadvantage of smaller numbers.

An arrow bounced off the back of Casca's armor. Several of his men had fallen. As the Olmecs reached Casca's casualties, those seriously wounded were speared to death; those who would live were held for the coming sacrifices.

As the Olmecs poured into the city their ranks were ever more congested by the width of the streets, forcing them to crowd in on one another in a great, uncontrollable mass.

The Olmec officers screamed in frustration, trying to get control of their men, but it was too late. The units were mixed. They were following only those directly in front of them. Behind the melee, riding his enormous litter, Teypetel entered the city bellowing for his men to kill, kill. In his excitement he took the whip from one of his slavemasters and lashed the backs of the litter slaves into bloody ribbons as they struggled and gasped through open mouths, laboring to carry the tremendous load of the litter with its obese passenger.

Casca's men had fallen back now to the front ranks of the waiting Serpent soldiers. Breathless, they found their way to the rear as the ranks opened to let them pass, then closed again. The oncoming wave of the Olmecs met the closed wall of the Serpents. The Olmecs stood for a moment frozen in time, face to face with the Teotec, unable to move. The oncoming ranks of the Olmecs then pushed their brothers against the Teotec line. The screams of the fighting masses of men flooded the air, drowning the death cries of those who fell.

The Vikings stood firm in the rear, their weapons ready. Holdbod the Berserker was almost beside himself with frustration. Swaying back and forth on his heels, he cried for Olaf to let him go, that he would kill enough for everyone. Tears running down his face in anguish, he obeyed Olaf's order to stand firm, but the strain on him was terrible.

The sheer weight of the Olmec masses was more than Casca's men could withstand. Step by step the Olmecs forced the Teotecs back—but now a rain of missiles began falling on them from the rooftops, from the force Casca had stationed there; the old ones were lending their support. A chamber pot still filled from last night's use broke the nose of an Olmec captain who broke into a frenzy as the filth ran into his mouth and down his chest. The old man responsible cackled and jumped up and down in glee. The protesting Olmec's agony was stilled by a flint-tipped spear pushing out the back of his skull.

Casca stood in the front ranks for a moment to let his soldiers see him, and with the aid of his *Gladius Iberius* he chopped off the heads of a dozen weapons and slew even more of the Olmecs, the thick-bladed Roman sword slicing through the thin armor of the Olmecs, laying chests and heads open.

The Olmecs in the front were sucking air through open mouths, laboring to breathe. The long run was taking its toll, but to the eyes of Totzin it appeared that the Olmecs were winning. After all, they were in the center of the city. He signaled to his men to join the Olmecs. They did, but these traitorous Jaguar soldiers of Teotah soon found themselves inextricably mixed with the Olmecs. Hundreds were cut down in the confusion by their new allies.

Totzin disappeared. . . .

The time was now.

Casca suddenly screamed orders above the clamor of battle.

The ranks of the Serpent soldiers immediately fell back on themselves, running to the rear to regroup, leaving a vacuum that the confused Olmecs filled.

The Olmecs halted, transfixed by the sight before them, the totally unexpected.

Giants.

Giants with shaggy faces and light-colored hair—wearing a shiny skin the Olmec's stone-tipped weapons bounced off without doing any damage. Terrible beings with shining weapons that sang above their heads and sliced through all who got in their way.

The Vikings.

Casca's "anvil," they stood rockline and solid and carved the men opposing them into unrecognizable facsimiles of humanity. The Olmec spirit broke at the indestructibility of these fearsome apparitions who uttered strange cries to strange gods . . . "Odin!" . . . "Thor!" and shouted "Casca! Casca! Casca" as they moved forward, a knot of steel before which everything died. In their terror the Olmecs broke and began to fight their way back down the long thoroughfare—anything to get away from this place of slaughter. In their frenzied rush to get away, those in front killed those behind. The panic spread like wildfire. The Olmec units collapsed in on themselves. Thousands were trampled underfoot as their brothers fought to get away from the horrible shining ones behind them.

The Vikings were magnificent. Foremost in the field of slaughter were Olaf and Vlad. They blocked the thrusts of spears and stone-edged clubs with their shields. They parried and thrust and chopped and sliced through everything in their path.

And then Holdbod the Berserker leaped in front, jumping over a pile of dead Olmecs.

The manic rage was upon him. Nothing could stop him now in his desire for blood. He raced out into the heavy mass of retreating Olmecs crying for Thor to give him strength to kill more and more. His great sword rained a destruction upon the Olmecs such as they had never imagined could exist. Endlessly he killed. An Olmec captain leaped in front of this monster to stop him. Holdbod wrapped his great arms around the man as he would a child and through tear-filled eyes thanked Odin for this gift, alternately crying and laughing, he snuggled the smaller form of the Olmec against his chest and squeezed, unmindful of the Olmecs trying to tear him loose from their captain. The Olmec chieftain gave a long ululating strangling cry as his ribs collapsed and crushed in on themselves, his head back in an arc of pain. Holdbod squeezed the life out of him, not feeling the cuts from the obsidian blades or the half-dozen arrows protruding from his back. He dropped the Olmec, regained his sword, and the great blade began to swing again . . . up and down . . . up and down . . . endlessly.

Casca joined him, his short sword doing equal, if not quite as bloody, work. Casca was sparing in his strokes, making each one count, while Holdbod fought mindlessly. He even turned on Casca, knocking his leader to the ground and standing over him, his great sword raised above his head ready to slice this fallen foe to separate pieces. A hand grasped his wrist. "Brother, hold." Vlad the Dark's quiet voice broke the blood film around Holdbod's mind. Looking down at Casca and recognizing him, Holdbod began to sob uncontrollably.

Casca got to his feet and hugged Holdbod's hairy shoulder. "No fear, brother. It's not my time. Now, go and rest. Leave some of them for the rest of us."

Still sobbing, Holdbod walked unseeing to the rear. The rage had come and gone. Only his wounds were unfelt. The arrows in his back waved and bobbed up and down like some obscene gesturing.

Once to the rear, he fell unconscious.

Vlad took his place in the forefront, his great axe doing at least double duty. If anything the quiet intensity of this deadly stranger struck even greater fear into the hearts of the already panic-stricken Olmecs. All semblance of order disappeared in their ranks. Blind panic ruled now. Teypetel had lashed his bearers until they had collapsed, spilling their load into the street of death. Rising, the greasy, bulbous monster tried to stop the blind retreat of his legions, cutting down man after man with his copper blade, but to no avail. They streamed past him in mindless terror.

"Dog fucker, I am here."

Turning, Teypetel, god and king of the Olmecs, faced Casca the stranger and god from the sea. A chill ran through his bowels. Was this a god? Before he could answer his own question, Casca was upon him, his blade slicing away the haft of Teypetel's axe. Teypetel, god of the Olmecs, wet himself as he turned to flee. Casca threw his Roman short sword at the back of the terrified king, knocking him to the earth already sticky and claylike with the blood of thousands of his followers.

Casca grasped the bald head of the downed king and raised him to his knees. Placing his own knee in the Olmec's back along the spine, he pulled the grotesque head back. "Well, you piece of shit, it's time for you to meet your ancestors." Casca placed his scarred, sinewy hands together, interlocking the fingers. The butt of a hand on each side of the obese king's temples, he began to squeeze. As he pushed in, taking ever deeper breaths, the muscles in his own back snapped and crackled with the strain. But the tremendous pressure was being transmitted to the king's brain case. Teypetel squirmed and sobbed, promising anything if only the Quetza would stop squeezing.

His answer came, quicker than he had expected —but not in the way he wanted it. With one great expulsion of air the skull of the king of the Olmecs cracked along the fracture lines—like the shell of a turtle—and began to cave in upon itself, sharp pieces of the brain case knifing into the living brain itself. The the whole skull gave way and Casca's hands were holding only a reddish gray, bleeding mass of bone and ruptured brain tissue.

Several Olmec captains had been looking back, already terrified by the pursuing Teotec and their fearsome allies. When they witnessed Casca's gruesome dispatch of their former king, that was the final straw. No longer trying to maintain even the semblance of cohesion, they fled blindly back the way they had come, every man for himself, leaving thousands of their brothers dead or in the process of being put into that state by the avenging Teotec. Even the old men and old women had descended from the rooftops to aid in this effort. The old women especially seemed to delight in bashing the brains out of wounded Olmecs. Compassion was a commodity reserved for their own.

Wiping his hands on his cuirass, Casca grimaced distaste of the clinging pieces of bone and brain tissue. The Vikings had stopped following the retreating enemy and were now involved in looting the bodies of the fallen. Thinking nothing of such activity—since it was standard battle practice—Casca decided he had better find Metah and see how she had made out. He had lost all thought of her when word of the advancing Olmecs had reached him. Stepping over the bodies of both Olmec and Teotec soldiers he started to make his way back down the thoroughfare. Periodically he would bend over the body of a fallen Viking, imprint the man's name and face in his memory, close his eyes for a moment, then move on. They had died the way they would have wished. It was fortunate that no more had fallen than had. Entering the great square, Casca automatically looked up the pyramid where only a few months before he had felt the golden flint knife cut into him. Involuntarily he shivered, and turned to go to his own palace.

"Quetza!"

The booming voice of Tezmec froze Casca in his tracks. Taking off his plumed helmet, he shaded his eyes and looked to the source of the calling.

On the temple at the top of the pyramid Tezmec stood in full priestly dress, his robes whipping around him from the breeze, his body painted coal black, bright carmelian red circles drawn around his eyes.

"Quetza!" The old man's voice boomed stronger than Casca had ever heard. "You have brought this upon us." The old man waved to the masses of dead below. "You have brought this tragedy to my people. You are a false god. I told you we must have messengers to go to the heavens and deliver our prayers, but you would not have it so. Instead my people lie dead in our streets. This is your doing. You are no god. You cannot even protect your own woman. Totzin has taken her." Tezmec indicated the road leading to the high mountains. "False god, you will stop me from doing my duty no longer.

The gods will have a messenger, and perhaps then our curse will be lifted."

Tezmec held above his head the same shining blade that he had used on Casca.

The Roman noticed for the first time that the altar fires were lit and smoke was rising from the flames.

"I shall do my duty," the old man repeated.

In less than a heartbeat's time the ancient priest slashed his own chest open, exposing the cavity. Casca felt a pain in his own chest. He knew exactly what the old priest was feeling. The old man raised his face to the heavens and cried, his voice breaking in agony for his people: "O gods of my fathers, Quetza, Tlaloc, hear my prayers and forgive your children for they know not what they do. Accept me in payment for their sins." The old man threw his body onto the flames of the altar. His open chest, right over the center of the fire, sizzled and crackled. Tezmec screamed not once, for he was dead before the fire touched him. There was only silence as the flames consumed the insides of his body and turned his old heart into a shriveled cinder.

Silence lay over the city. All had stopped. Casca was stunned. What had the old man said about forgiveness and sins? Where had he heard that before?

Metah! Did he say that little runt Totzin had Metah? Not stopping, Casca began running in the direction Tezmec had pointed, out past the city's edge, out through the spiny maguey fields. He ran one step after another, eyes straining to see ahead.

That poisonous little shit had Metah. . . .

THIRTEEN

Metah's hands were bound behind her with a strip of rawhide. A leash of the same was around her throat, cutting off her breath every time she stumbled or faltered. Totzin jerked and cursed as he dragged her along, relentlessly trying to reach the hidden sanctuary in the distant mountains, the sanctuary only he knew of. There he would be safe and gather to himself the loyal survivors of his cult. From there he would build his own city and grow in strength until he could return and take vengeance. Everything had gone wrong. How could the Olmecs have lost?

Metah stumbled and lay still. Viciously jerking her leash, he commanded her to rise and walk. The cord twisted itself and cut a thin red line in her brown flesh.

Struggling to her knees, she looked the Jaguar priest straight in the face. "No. I will go no further, eater of filth, traitor."

Totzin struck her with the back of his hand. "Silence, you she-slut. You will obey."

Metah's tongue touched the cut in her mouth, tasting salty blood.

"No further. I will go no further. Casca will come for me."

Instinctively Totzin looked back down from the ridge they were on. His body was old, but he had the eyes and vision of youth. A movement in the corner of his eyes caused him to focus on something in the distance. At first he thought it might have been a deer, but light sparkling off the body told him it was Casca. The strange armor was what was shining. *The bitch is right. The devil comes. How did he know which way we had gone?*

Smiling a snaggle-toothed grin, he said, "Well, enough. I will give him what he wants and slow him up enough that I may escape."

Pulling Metah to him by the sheer force of his jerking on the leather leash, he dragged her across sharp stones and cactus spines. Taking her by the back of her long black hair, he forced her head up and faced her toward where Casca was coming.

"You're right, bitch. He comes, and I shall see that he is not disappointed, for surely he wants you more than I do. There will be plenty for me to satisfy myself with when I am away. Therefore I leave you to him."

Metah gasped as a burning pain set her abdomen on fire. Consciousness mercifully left her. . . .

Totzin wiped the blade of his obsidian dagger across his tongue, tasting the sweet salty richness of her blood. He had an extraordinary knowledge of anatomy due to the thousands he had sent to his

Jaguar god. He had stabbed her low, just above the pubic hair. It would take long for her to die, perhaps even days. The foreign devil, her lover, would surely stop to care for her, and he would make good his escape to his sanctuary. Leaving the injured Metah behind, he gave one more look to where Casca was easily visible now, leaping over bushes and rocks in his path, closer than Totzin would have thought. The priest ran, losing himself in the scrub trees and brush, trying to get away from the devil from the sea. He ran as fast as his thin legs could take him away from that butchering madman.

Casca almost stepped on the huddled mass that was Metah. His heart stopped for a moment, and with a cry of anguish he dropped beside her body and gently turned her over. A small coughing like that of a hurt child brought a rush of relief to him. *She lives. . .* Cutting her bonds, he cradled her in his arms and began to walk down the hills. No thought of Totzin or vengeance was in his mind, only Metah and her pain. Quickly, swiftly, careful not to jar her as he walked, he brought her home. The sun had gone behind the rim of mountains surrounding the valley when he brought her to his palace. None spoke. One look at his face was enough to stop all questioning.

That night while he sat watching her, cooling her face with a damp rag, he suffered again the pains of losing someone he loved. His silent care and thoughts were interrupted by a presence. A young shaman of the Coyote clan stood in the doorway. Silently he walked across the tiled floor to the bed. Gently he took the rag from Casca's hand, and bending over he looked at the wound. He inspected the point of entrance. Gently his fingers touched and probed around the area of the wound. Only once did Metah moan when he touched her. His wrist was quickly locked in a steel vise as Casca grabbed and held him. The young priest gently and determinedly took Casca's hand from his wrist.

"Tectli Quetza, she dies."

The young priest's voice was soft but certain.

"The cut is deep inside. For years I have watched and studied. It has come to me that when one has lost too much of his blood, he dies. I have seen many like her. When the blood leaves the body or fills the abdomen, they weaken; the heart beats faster, but weaker. They go into a deep sleep as she has now and do not wake. She will die before the dawn."

Casca groaned at the young man's words.

"Is there no hope? No way to save her?"

The young priest nodded. "One perhaps, Tectli. But before I explain it to you, let me say that I do not agree with the priest Tezmec. The Olmecs would have come sooner or later. Under torture the Jaguar priest Totzin's men have confessed their treachery."

Casca nodded. "Well, that's something at least. Perhaps then all the blame is not mine. But still this is. She is my woman, and what has happened to her is my responsibility. That I do know. If you can do anything to save her, young priest, then do it now, and do it before she leaves me."

"As you command, Tectli. My name is Sactle. All my life I have wondered what is death and what is the cause of death. There are many things that cause it, but one, as I told you, is when too much of the body's blood is lost. I believe that the blood is the life force of all. I have experimented with many animals—including monkeys, whose bodies are amazingly like man's in their construction. I once let the blood out of one and put back in the blood of another when the beast was close to death as is your lady Metah now. The blood of the second monkey kept the first from dying. The secret of life, Tectli, I believe is in the blood."

Casca thought for a moment.

In the blood. . . . Perhaps he is right. It was the blood of the Jew that caused my condition, my being condemned to live and never age. Perhaps if I gave Metah some of my blood the life force that sustains me would save her also. . . . Hope rose in him. *She might even become as me! At last I would have someone to walk through the ages with me until the Jew sets me free! Not to be alone anymore . . . to be able to stay with one person and not to have to look for signs of fear in their faces when their hair turns to gray and wrinkles show the passage of time and I remain the same. . . . Yes, it must be the blood.*

Aloud he said: "Do it, priest. Do it now before she is too weak to help. And use my blood to fill her with life."

The Coyote priest bowed. "As you wish, Tectli. But know that I can promise nothing. Never have I tried this on humans. It may not succeed. But she will die if nothing is done. That I swear to."

"Then be about it, man." Casca's voice rose. "Make haste while we still have time. You said she would die before dawn. That leaves us less than an hour if we do nothing."

Sactle took from his pouch a long thin flexible strip of material.

"What the Hades is that?" Casca demanded in irritation.

Sactle answered, "It is made from the sap of a tree that grows to the south. We also make a ball from it that we play with in the courtyards. I take the sap and smear it over a small reed. It is hardened in the fire, in the heat from the smoke. When it is ready, it is pulled back and rolled off the reed leaving a flexible tube. It is through this that your blood will pass from you to your lady."

He reached again into his pouch and took out two golden needles, showing them to Casca.

"These, too, are hollow. They will fit into the ends of the sap tubing. I will insert one of the needles into your arm, into one of the channels through which your life's blood flows, and the other into that of the Lady Metah. Your body being the stronger, your blood force should push its way into her weakened system. Now, Tectli, lie down beside your lady."

Casca did as the priest said, putting his thick-muscled body next to the slight frame of the woman he loved. She looked even tinier . . . as though she were fading away. There were hollows under the eyes he remembered as having sparkled with life. Her cheeks had a starved look.

"Get on with it, priest."

"Patience, Tectli. It will take but a moment." Taking another strip of the flexible sap tubing, Sactle wrapped it around Casca's arm and tied a knot in it above Casca's elbow. "It will stop the flow of your blood to your arm until the needle is in your blood channel. Then the tube tie will be released, and the blood will flow again." He worked swiftly. Deftly he entered the needle into Casca's vein. Turning to Metah, he searched for a while, probing gently with the needle until he finally had it inserted in her.

"Now, Tectli, we release the tie."

Casca nodded. Watching Metah's face, he never noticed the priest letting the tie around his upper arm loose. It wasn't until he felt the tingling that meant the blood flow was returning that he noticed it. The priest held the open end of the tubing away from Metah. It had not been attached to the golden needle in her arm. Drops of Casca's blood began to drip out of the end of the tube. Then a small steady stream.

"You fool!" Casca cursed the priest. "Why haven't you attached the needle?"

The priest merely looked quietly at Casca. "Because, Tectli, I have found that I must wait until the blood fills the tube before transferring it. Otherwise a quantity of air will be transmitted in front of the blood. For some reason I do not know this is a fatal thing to have happen. Now!" He attached the open end of the flexible tube to the needle in Metah's arm.

Casca watched her face intently, concentrating on willing her to live. He saw the progress of the blood, watching the flow increase the weak pulse in her throat. Seconds passed. Metah stirred. Slowly the pulse in her throat quickened.

"It's working, Sactle! It's working!"

Metah stirred more strongly.

Her eyes snapped open.

She screamed.

She screamed over and over, ever louder and louder, then weaker.

A dark flush ran up her face, turning her once-beautiful features into a contorted mask. She screamed once more, one final cry that faded into nothingness as her face turned black and she died, mouth open, eyes unseeing.

"No!" Casca cried. "What's wrong? What's happened? Why did she die?"

Sactle backed away from Casca, fear written in his face.

He made a sign to ward off the evil eye.

His voice quivered:

"Your blood . . . it's poison. Deadly poison. I have seen the same thing happen when one has been bitten by a poisonous snake. You are the Quetza! Your blood is poison—for you are a god!"

The priest prostrated himself.

"Forgive me, Tectli, for I had doubted your divinity. Now no one can deny it. Forgive me. . . .

Unnoticed, he crawled out of Casca's presence.

Casca wept, tears running down his face. He cried as a child would, uncontrollably, as if trying to purge himself of grief and pain in one tremendous outpouring of anguish.

"I have killed you, Metah! My blood has killed you! If another had given it to you, you would have lived. I gave you mine seeking to give you eternal life, but I gave you hell. Forgive me, Metah!"

Totzin climbed higher and higher. He was in the

pine forests of the mountains. The thick trees let the light of the moon break through, casting beams of silver on the forest floor. He made his way toward safety. Dawn was almost upon him. By noon he would be safe. He paused by a pine to catch his breath . . . and a familiar sound came to him.

The coughing roar of a hunting jaguar.

But not as men might imitate it. This was the full, vital, deadly cry of the jungle master, the killer.

Totzin froze, eyes wide. He searched the bushes around him. The jaguar was close. Silence. No sounds reached Totzin except that of his own labored breathing rasping in his ears. Then there was the soft whisper of brush cracking.

He saw it.

In the shadows, a spotted hide mottled black against the bushes.

The Jaguar.

The huge cat's eyes gleamed in the moonlight as it lowered its body to the ground, the tail whipping slowly back and forth. Nose black and shiny, the cat gathered itself, the great muscles bunching. It looked Totzin in the eye. Totzin could not move. His mouth opened.

"Mcht tl ley cotzli, Teypetel . . ." he whispered.

The cat cocked one ear, listening.

Again, louder, Totzin began the ancient chant of the cat god: "Mcht tl ley cotzli, Teypetel." Repeating the chant, Totzin lost his fear. After all, this was his god, and he its servant. He stepped forward, chanting louder, the beast seemingly understanding the ancient words. Totzin was elated. *The god heard and understood. . . .*

The thought that the god with the spotted hide

listened was still in his mind when the great cat sprung, but the words on his lips seemed far away; the sound of his bones being cracked between the cat's teeth was much louder.

Much louder. . .

So Totzin, high priest of the Jaguar, served his god well to the very end. His god enjoyed him to the fullest. Then, licking the blood from its muzzle, it dragged the remainder of the carcass to its lair where its cubs waited to be fed.

FOURTEEN

During the following days the Teotec captains consolidated their gains against the Olmec, taking hostages and having the successor to Teypetel swear allegiance and send tribute to pay for the damages the Olmec had done to the city. The Vikings buried their dead under massive stones in the hills, facing them out to the distant sea. The men's armor and weapons were not buried with them as was the normal custom. Steel was too precious a commodity to leave. Instead, the men were buried with weapons of the chiefs of the Teotec.

During this time Casca was not to be seen. He was sunk in black, deep grief and refused to be consoled by anyone. Only during Metah's funeral did he appear, to see that she was treated with the care of a queen. The entire city turned out in mourning for the occasion. The women wailed and slashed their faces with their nails. The men wore ashes on their bodies and somberly lined the funeral procession. She was taken to a hill outside where a tomb had been prepared filled with all the things she would need in the afterlife . . . pots and clothes, jewelry and toilet articles. At the burial, each article was in its turn broken so that its spirit could travel to the spirit world with her. Even the clothes were torn so that they could perform the same purpose. Twenty of the bravest of the Olmec warriors slain in the fight were laid in a semicircle at her feet, to be her slaves forever in the afterlife. A silver mask covered her face, and her hands were crossed over her bosom. Massive stones were laid about her, and their area swept clean. Trees were planted on the spot so no one could find it again.

Casca observed all this silently, rigid, without emotion—for he had been drained of all feeling.

The night following the funeral he made a decision.

Going to the chambers of the king Cuz-mecli, he called for the wise men and priests to hear his words. They gathered in one of the larger vaulted rooms of the palace, a room painted with brilliant frescoes.

Standing before the ones he had assembled, Casca gathered his thoughts, slowly picking every word he would say.

"Your majesty, wise men of the Teotec nation, listen to my words and pay heed. It has come to me that my time with you is at an end. The circle is complete. As I came to you from the sea, so I must return again to the sea. It is my fate, and the will of the gods."

Cuz-mecli started to protest.

"No, young king, it must be so. Now hear me. As

I have said, everything is a great circle, and all that was shall be again. So it shall. One day I will return. Watch for me to come from the sea. I brought you messages from the gods. Obey them. There shall be no more human sacrifices on your altars. Remove from all the paintings and artwork of your city any sign of human sacrifice. It is not needed. Though you may be sorely tried and tempted to resort to the old ways when bad times come upon you, do not fall to that temptation—if you fear the gods and my vengeance. The bad times will test to see if you obey."

One old shaman was nodding, his head apparently filled with the sleep of age. Suddenly his eyes snapped wide open, and he straightened, his rheumatoid hands clenched in gnarled fists. In a thin, crackling voice he spoke:

"Tectli, I have seen that what you say is true. You will come again with others, but the ships will not be of the dragon. They will have many sails, and the men will appear different, with skins of shining light. Marvelous beasts will do their bidding and carry them into battle so that they will appear to be half men and half animal, able to run like the wind and travel far. They will spread fire and death among those who still sacrifice on the altars. The people of the valley will be destroyed, but they will not be our people. Our city will long since have been covered by the forests and deserts, but our city will die peacefully and will obey your law.

"You shall return to the valley of the Teotec, but we shall be gone. Yet you shall be remembered. We shall send out holy men to tell of you and your coming. As you have said, the circle will be complete, and those who have not honored your command will perish. As a people and as a nation they shall be as dust. New ones will inherit all that was in the valley. In one reed, Tectli. It is so, and shall be."

The old man dropped into silence, his cheeks hollow, exhausted by his vision, breath rattling in his body chest. As Casca watched him, for just a blink of an eye a shadow seemed to settle over the Teotec shaman, and the features of Shiu Lao Tze seemed to smile out from him . . . then they vanished.

A weary Casca prepared to leave the chambers. But before he left he said, "In the morning, then, we shall leave. Farewell, and rule well, young king. You have the soul of greatness about you."

The Vikings cheered when Casca told them of their returning. Loud shouts of "Ave!" and "Hail, Casca!" rang out as they scurried to gather their possessions and loot.

The morning rose and the feel of the day was auspicious. The Vikings gathered as a company at the foot of the great pyramid that had known so much blood and pain. They waited, packs on their backs, weapons slung and scabbarded.

The great square was filled not only with the city people but also with those from the surrounding countryside. Shoulder to shoulder they waited, fathers holding their children on their shoulders so that they might see and remember this day for all their years.

Casca appeared on the pyramid in his feathered robe, Serpent headdress, and wearing the jade mask. He motioned with one hand. A line of two hundred porters advanced, each carrying a straw basket. These went before the Vikings, and several porters opened their loads to show the contents—gold, silver, jewels, and precious stones filled each basket to capacity. Just one basket would have made each Viking richer than his wildest dreams, and here were two hundred of them.

Calling out in the Norse tongue, Casca said to the men below:

"There is your reward as I promised."

The Vikings started to break and run for the precious baskets, but were quickly snapped back in ranks by a harsh word from Olaf.

The drums began to beat, a sharp, distinct pattern. With each stroke Casca took a step and began his descent from the pyramid. The bindings of the jade mask again felt as if they were cutting into his face. He peered out the eyeholes as if through a tunnel. The scar on his chest burned. He reached the bottom, and the people of the city bowed in homage to the god Quetza. One small child, about three, ran forward and took his hand, bright, fearless eyes looking up into those of Casca behind the mask. The boy's mother came forward to jerk the boy back, but was stopped by a sign from Casca. Bending over, he picked the boy up and put him on his shoulders, and the three-year-old Teotec squealed with pleasure. The sound of the child's laughter broke the tension, and all began to cheer and sing in happy voices. The day had changed from one of sorrow to one of promise.

Casca strode along, his steps picking up speed as if by the trust of the child he was being relieved of the pain that was Metah and the grief was put to rest. He went to the entrance of the great hall. Setting the boy down and taking the child's small hand in his larger paw, he walked inside past braziers burning incense to where the only decorations were the six masks hanging on the walls.

A bent figure stepped forward and bowed. It was Pletuc the carver. Now Casca remembered him as the one who had broken the Olmec captain's nose with the chamber pot full of night soil, and he smiled. Taking the mask from his face, he walked to the place prepared for it on the day of his sacrifice. Slowly, carefully, he set the mask with the others and stepped back, looking at his own face in motionless, timeless jade . . . true to the smallest detail. Even the hairline scar left on him by the Greek whore was perfect. He glanced at the old carver.

"I told you I would hang the mask in the hall with my own hands."

The carver chuckled. "So you did, Tectli. And it does look very good there hanging with the others." The old man walked to the display with pride. As if he personally owned the masks here he pointed to each one and called it by name. His great-grandfather had carved the first two, his father the next three, and he had been honored with the duty of carving the likeness of Cuz-mecli's father, the king—and the even greater honor of carving this last one, this likeness of the living god, the Quetza. He paused, and then spoke, his reedy voice piping:

"Something is missing."

"What's that, old one?"

"These." Pletuc showed two gray-blue ovals.

Taking the mask of Casca down, he worked with the jade for a moment and then put it back on its hanger. "There. It is complete." The jade mask seemed to have taken on life. The old man had inserted two carved eyes of the same shade and hue as Casca's. The jade mask lived. "It needs eyes to watch over your city, Tectli. Now it shall see all."

Pleased with himself, Casca grinned. "It's good, old man, but I'll wager you I shall wear the mask again when this city is gone from memory."

Cackling, Pletuc laughed. "No, Tectli. I do not wager. You won the last time you said you would do something. I did not get this old by wagering on things I could not collect on."

Casca laughed with him and swung the young boy back on his shoulders. Tousling the child's hair, he said to him, "I would give all the years of all the centuries and the wealth of great nations to one such as you to be my son. Will you be my son?"

The three-year-old smiled timidly, and though he did not understand the meaning of Casca's words, his trust in this strange man was so complete that he bobbed his head in an affirmative manner.

"Good. Then so it shall be. For am I not a god? And are not the words of a god law?" He carried the boy out into the bright day where the masses of Teotah waited. Raising the child above his head, he boomed out: "Hear me! This is my son. I adopt him." The boy's mother had a look of confused panic. Was she going to lose her son?

Casca looked her straight in the eyes and said gently, "Fear not. I leave him in your care. Take him back to the city. But from this day this child shall carry my name. He will be called the Quetza.

Not a god, but a man. Remember, he is mine. Take care of him."

Striding to where his Vikings waited, Casca took from himself the feathered robe of green and gave it to Cuz-mecli. "Grow into this, young king, and rule wisely, for I shall be watching." He touched the boy's cheek with approval. Then he put on his Roman armor, drew his sword, and pointed east. "To the ships! We sail for the Hold . . . and home."

The Vikings roared in approval. Olaf stepped forward, the first step, and they all followed. They marched escorted by a guard of one thousand Serpent warriors. Holdbod refused the litter ordered for him. Even with his sore back he marched beside Olaf and Vlad. "The way to the sea is for men to walk, and not be carried like babies," he grumbled.

The way to the sea was pleasant. Casca and his men were honored wherever they stopped. Food was always ready—and willing maidens added some bloodlines to their tribes. Casca, though, refused all women. Metah was still too close.

The hills gave way to jungle. And finally to one last rise. Here Casca led the way and pointed down. "The sea. We are here."

His men spent that night in revelry, telling the story of their adventures to those left behind on the ships, filling them with envy that was soon dispersed when those who had to remain behind were shown the baskets of wealth of which they would receive a full share. The next morning the ships were hauled back into the surf and lay at anchor. Supplies were loaded all that day and the next. The ships swung on their anchors as if eager to be off from these strange waters and to return to the more familiar fjords where they were born.

When the ships were loaded and the tide favorable, Casca bade farewell to the escorting Serpent soldiers and sent them back to their city where so much had happened to him and to them, then he returned to the ship. The Vikings were ready. The cargo was stowed. Casca stood at the tiller. The sun reflected silver spots on the small waves.

"Set oars and begin the stroke!" he ordered. "We sail for home."

The oars sliced into the water and the dragon ships began to move, slowly at first, and then with greater speed. They entered the open waters and turned north. North, back the long way they had come. Many of their brothers would not make this voyage with the Vikings, but surely they were already in Valhalla drinking and boasting of their feats in this strange land of temples and birds. Wassail would be sung for the dead when the Vikings returned to home fires. The striped red and white sails were set. They filled. The wind was now the master. The dragon ships rode like well-trained stallions, sliding and slipping through the waters, homeward bound.

The night was warm, but the sails were filled, and the bows of the dragon ships cut through the phosphorescent water. In the leading ship, Casca, forward, looked across the dark waters.

Home . . . he thought. *Where is home for me? Everyone else has a place to which he belongs. I do not. . . .*

Beyond the silver phosphorescence of the bow wave the sea waters were black . . . like death. . . .

Would that I could lose myself in you. . . . Would that the wetness might cover me forever. Surely everything must end in time . . . and my time cannot be much longer. . . .

Moving his hand against the smooth railing, he muttered aloud:

"When will it end?"

A shiver ran over him as the Jew's voice came, unbidden:

"Till we meet again . . ."

FIFTEEN

"Sir . . . sir!" The voice was insistent. It was as if the lights had been turned on. Goldman turned to the voice. He saw Johnson, the museum guard, standing there with a confused look on his face.

"Are you all right, sir?" Johnson asked. "You've been standing there for hours. Your friend said that you weren't to be disturbed, that you were studying the article. But it's closing time now, and we have to shut up until tomorrow. You can come back then if you haven't finished examining the mask."

Goldman's mouth was dry. *Closing time. That meant he had been here seven hours.* "Yes. Thank you." He read the guard's metal name plate. "Thank you, Mr. Johnson. Yes. I'm quite all right, thank you. May I have just one more moment, please—alone? Then I'll leave."

Johnson nodded. "All right. But five minutes more is all I can let you have." Leaving Goldman, he shook his head. *What the hell could be so interesting about an old jade mask from Mexico?*

These brain types. I'll never figure them out. How can they stand in one spot for hours looking at something that doesn't move or talk? Just sits there. Well, that's their business. . . .

Not waiting until the guard had left, Goldman had turned back to the mask. Where had Casca gone this time? Would he return? *Somehow, Casca, I think we will meet again. I don't believe you've yet finished what you started.*

He gave one last look at the jade mask. It seemed to mock him. The thin hairline scar running from the corner of the left eye to the mouth gave the immobile jade the same slightly sardonic look as Casca . . . as if it knew a secret . . . some as yet untold joke.

Goldman straightened, twisting his head to ease the stiffness in his neck.

He left the museum, the closing doors separating him from another world.

As Goldman was leaving, another man was standing in a line waiting to get airline tickets that would take him from Boston to Johannesburg and from there to Salisbury in Rhodesia. As he stood, patiently, he checked his papers, including the Spanish passport identifying him as Carlos Romano, of Sevilla. Everything was in order. He nodded wearily. Several people in the line tried to put some distance between themselves and the man with the scarred face, but he didn't notice.